SERIAL

KILLER

GARRY JOHNSON

D1493938

NEW HAVEN PUBLISHING LTD

First Edition
Published 2017
NEW HAVEN PUBLISHING LTD
www.newhavenpublishingltd.com
newhavenpublishing@gmail.com

Cover design©Pete Cunliffe
pcunliffe@blueyonder.co.uk

newhaven
publishing

For my children

Sam, Adam and Lucy

Also By This Author

Boys Of The Empire

View From The Deadend Of The Street

The Gary Glitter Story

David Bowie Tribute

Ozzy Osbourne Story

Paul Young Story

The Queen Story

Till Death Us Do Part

Punk Rock Stories And Tabloid Tales

The Cockney Bard

Content

INTRODUCTION

For decades now, serial killers have taken centre-stage in the news and entertainment media. The coverage of real-life murderers such as Dennis Nilsen and Ted Bundy has transformed them into ghoulish celebrities. But never before has a serial killer personally known all her victims.

Taylor Shelley was a mass murderer who genuinely believed she had a right to kill. As she admitted in police interviews, the murders were not random, they were personal.

Days before her arrest, Taylor gave a world exclusive interview to tabloid journalist Rebekah Woods. The pair bonded immediately and agreed to co-operate on the book you are now reading.

Taylor says:

"This is the true story of my time at Gable Brook Comprehensive. A snapshot of incidents I recall taking place over a six year period"

12th September 2016 The Independent newspaper reported:

Six out of 10 girls and women aged 13 to 21 had faced sexual harassment at school or college.

An alarming report by a House of Commons committee condemns what it calls the 'shocking scale' of the problem, with pupils routinely touched sexually and called 'sluts' or 'slags'.

More worryingly, schools and teachers are failing to report incidents or take them seriously

Adding:

Schools should be safe places and no young person should suffer harassment or violence

A British Government Report published in November 2016 stated:
Sexual abuse of girls is 'accepted as part of everyday life' and the rise of the 'lad culture' means teachers are effectively 'condoning sexual harassment'

The official document called it a new trend. New fashion and music are trends. Sexual abuse is not a trend, it's a violent crime and sadly nothing new. Unlike politicians and social workers, Taylor Shelley is an expert on the subject.

A genuine victim who until now suffered in silence:
"In the 1980s I attended an Essex Comprehensive where bad things happened every day. I was just an object, and saying 'No' wasn't a option".

The NSPCC states:
A child is sexually abused when they are forced or persuaded to take part in sexual activities

Payback was brutal and bloody. The only way Taylor could kill the pain was to wipe out the source. It had to be ice cold revenge, a final solution with Old Testament 'an eye for an eye' justice. Her life ruined by what 8 teenage boys had done to her, Taylor is determined to carve a path of revenge that will take each of them down. She is a woman seeking vengeance and goes on the rampage. Taylor Shelley becomes a serial killer.

ONE

The Police Interview

Taylor told D.I Charlotte Hawkins:

"I knew the net was closing in some 72 hours before my arrest. I contacted tabloid journalist Rebekah Woods and confessed. We booked into a Central London hotel and for the next two days I sung like a Canary. It was immediately obvious to Rebekah that I wasn't just another time-wasting fantasist. I didn't just know a lot about the killings, I had proof of my involvement. Gruesome photographs. I'd taken snapshots of Tory MP Paul Greening, Peter Brown and Terry Reason moments after I'd killed them. I also revealed detailed information about some of the other murders that hadn't been published in the media.

"Rebekah knew she was talking to a genuine serial killer, with more victims than Moors Murderer Myra Hindley and sexual deviant Rose West. She was excited. I wasn't just a mass murderer but the newest member of a rare breed, a female serial killer. I think she was a bit scared of me when she turned up with her minder, a great big muscular bloke she called Titch. She needn't have bothered. I wasn't killing randomly, there was a reason for what I did. But I silently accepted Titch's presence and he was smart enough to keep his mouth shut.

"Rebekah was soon aware she had a best-selling book to go with her world exclusive interview. I was box office, a tabloid sensation, as everyone is fascinated by women who kill, aren't they? Without blowing my own trumpet, I was without doubt the biggest scoop of her career. To ensure a TV documentary followed, she filmed my confession and took various photographs of me looking scary, sexy, moody and smiling. In some I looked like a serial killer, in others a model from an Anne Summers catalogue. As a top tabloid journalist, Rebekah knew what would sell papers and insured my face was splashed across the covers of magazines. At my request there were none of me crying or looking vulnerable. I refused to fake regret. No photo captured me showing remorse. I'd rather be hated then pitied.

"I was proud of what I'd done because I was no longer a silent victim. The bible says 'an eye for a eye' and that's exactly how I saw it. If it was good enough for God and religious leaders of various faiths to quote, then why not the same justice for Taylor Shelley?

"From the very first moment I opened my mouth, Rebekah was like a Lottery winner who'd hit the jackpot. I was her ticket to fame and fortune. I wasn't just a serial killer I had slaughtered a well-known Tory politician. A pillar of the establishment. A right-wing bigot. Voters didn't know about his violent past as a teenage gang leader and rapist. He was both the Jimmy Saville and Gary Glitter of politics.

"Rebekah wanted to follow-up the interview with an authorized autobiography. I agreed, on one condition. I wanted her to start the book off right, with both a strong opening and confession, to make sure it set the right tone, connected with the reader, and hopefully won some over to my side. Rebekah listened and her face was blank, never giving me a hint of how she felt about the deeds I had done. Titch, however, didn't seem to have her stamina and I could easily read the shock and horror on his face as my story unfolded. I wanted to show all the other people who'd been wronged in life how easy it was to get even, and prove it's never too late to right a wrong. If Titch's reactions were anything to go by, we had our work cut out for us.

"Technically it wasn't a politically motivated crime or traditional crime of passion, though I saw it as both. As a life-long feminist, I saw myself as a modern-day heroine for teenage girls. A pin-up for women around the world who were being bullied, sexually abused and persecuted by men.

"I didn't want people to love me, but to understand why I'd killed eight times. I wanted the court of public opinion on my side, or at least to give me the benefit of the doubt. I knew my trial would be a media sensation and an international news event. When I walked into the dock at the Old Bailey there would be reporters from around the world, armed police, curious onlookers and shell-shocked relatives. It would be the Taylor Shelley Show, the soap opera, and would rival the historic show trials of The Kray Twins, The Great Train Robbers, and Ruth Ellis.

"When I finished talking, Rebekah predicted that Hollywood would also want to film my story.

"The queen of Fleet Street was convinced she had hit the jackpot, Titch's face was drained of blood, white and pasty. He was obviously not as strong as Rebekah, but then I guess few people are."

Rebekah tells the police about her impressions of Taylor and what happened:

"I could see Taylor was a woman with exceptional poise. Self-control and had no intention of losing it. She said to me right at the start `you are not going to see me cry or hear me say sorry`. Of course I didn't want to make her cry. I just wanted a good headline and `I`ve no regrets` is much stronger than her saying `I`m sorry`.

"She was front page news and I wanted to be part of it. A great amount would be written, but nobody was better qualified to tell her story, and she had chosen to tell it to me. I wanted her authentic version published in my paper

"I was a seasoned tabloid journalist and knew it would give me a lot of airtime and earn me a fortune. That`s why I got her to sign on the dotted line and make me her official spokesman. I`d done PR for Rock stars, models, soap stars and footballers but this was my first Serial Killer.

"A few hours before our first meeting, she telephoned the office, and asked to see me as soon as possible. She said it`s urgent and seemed excited and suggested we meet at a West End hotel. I knew it was going to be a long night when she said `bring your pyjamas`.

"I took our security with me. No way was I walking into a hotel room alone with a self-confessed serial killer.

"Taylor opened the door looking as if she`d just walked off the set of a Hollywood movie. She was truly stunning, with an aura about her."

TWO

The Early Years

Taylor appeared to have everything in life, great looks, good career and luxury lifestyle. But how well did her friends and family really know her? From the outside, Taylor's life seemed pretty perfect. But her past is far from normal or happy. The 47-year-old blue-eyed blonde with the Amanda Holden figure and Kate Moss hair has it all. A successful and independent female admired by women and adored by men. But her past will shock you to the bone, so much so, many will understand her lust for revenge. Everybody has to draw a line in the sand some time. And for Taylor that time was now.

"The passing years hadn't healed me, memories hadn't faded and I was still woken by nightmares. I am a very pragmatic person and wear my heart on my sleeve, so therapy is not something I ever thought I would have to do, but I had run out of options. I sought professional help for 6 months but it didn't give me the tools to cope. As with my use of alcohol and drugs it wasn't enough to erase my past.

"In my mid-forties, I was still using cocaine to survive, just as I used cannabis as a teenager. I smoked weed to numb me from the constant harassment I received from Greening and his gang.

THE TEENAGE GANG:
   Leader: Paul Greening,
John Hunter, Billy Bishop, Peter Brown, Dave Barron,
Casey Newton, Terry Reason, David Reynolds.

"They were the tough boys, the cool guys, so I was bombarded with tormenting taunts from their mates and girlfriends. I was not popular. I was the underdog and alone, so I stayed silent and tried to block it out by self-medicating, and fake as much dignity as I could. There were years of drug abuse, heavy drinking, promiscuity, celibacy, and lesbian flings before I had peace of mind. Committing murder was the key to happiness. In all honesty I was messed up until I carried out my first murder."

Revenge is a dish best served cold, and a key motive for criminal activity. After all, who hasn't had the urge to get even? Most of us rise above it, but for some the impulse is just too great.

"I had been gang raped 3 times, twice as a juvenile and once as an adult. The first attacks involved five boys. The third was worse, as the boys were now men and this time there were eight attackers. It was not a gang bang. I hate that description of a violent crime. It was gang rape. Horrible, evil, nasty, cowardly, criminal and unforgiveable. I was not a willing participant like some adult actress in a porn movie. I was raped. I was not a member of the gang. I was the only person in the room who didn't want to be there. It scared me forever. Not for one moment did they consider the impact it would have on my life. It didn't occur to them.

"Since it happened, I've despised and hated them all with every fibre of my body. Paul Greening in particular took perverse pleasure in my suffering"

The final attack lasted more than 3 hours, and the things they did are burned into her memory. The constant laughing, endless threats and verbal abuse was almost as bad as the actual rapes. Nobody but him could make her feel as totally worthless and helpless.

"I knew there had to be some form of retribution, and thought killing him would provide some semblance of closure. Greening ruined my life, now I would end his. I became a cold blooded serial killer but didn't see myself as a criminal. I was just a victim, fighting back."

THREE

This is a Modern World

At the start of 1979, few people like 11-year-old Taylor Shelley would even have heard of Mods. A full scale Mod revival inspired by the band The Jam had exploded on to the youth scene in London and spread into the suburbs, and although it had its roots in 1979, it was certainly 1980 that was the year of the Mod revival.

It was also the year Taylor moved schools and first met Paul Greening. A racist skinhead three years older than her, and with two elder brothers to back him up, Greening struck both fear and blind loyalty into his mates. He was the school bully who led an eight-strong gang of teenage tearaways. Unlike his followers he still wore bovver boots, shaved his head and worshipped Adolf Hitler.

Greening wasn't smart enough to understand Weller's lyrics, or sharp enough to wear a mohair suit. He was many things, but definitely not a dedicated follower of fashion. His only concession to Mod was indulging in amphetamine. His gang wore Harrington jackets and button down shirts with two-tone trousers, loafers or brogues. He still swaggered about in a battered A1 combat jacket with rolled-up jeans and Doc Martens. The Mod revival's mainstream popularity was relatively short, although its influence has lasted for decades. Everyone from Oasis to Blur was influenced by Mod culture, be it Paul Weller or 60's originals like The Small Faces.

Musically, Greening was also out of tune with the gang of Mods who followed him. As well as The Jam, they were into 2-Tone bands like The Specials and The Selecter. Much to the annoyance of their leader, they also liked dancing to Tamla-Motown and Prince Buster. Greening was not only out of date when it came to fashion but stone deaf when it came to music and loved racist talentless bands like Screwdriver. Do you get the picture I'm painting? Paul Greening was not a nice boy. Even the teachers were scared of him, so what chance did I have against a sex pest in bovver boots?"

Taylor came into contact with Greening on day one at her new school.

"We'd moved from East London to Stanhope, a new town in Essex, because my Dad hated all the immigrants. He was worried about me having a black boyfriend, or worse, in his mind, a black baby. I remember him freaking out when I put a Bob Marley poster on my bedroom wall. I will tell you more about my dad later.

"According to my mum, within hours of him ripping it up they were sitting in the Estate Agents.

"My dad was very old-fashioned and a bigot. A self-confessed fascist who thought voting National Front was patriotic. He boasted of marching alongside East End dockers in support of Enoch Powell.

"Every August Bank Holiday he'd pray for rain, hoping it would ruin the Notting Hill Carnival. I was quite nervous about my first day at a new school even though my mum told me 'Cockney sparrows are scared of nothing and no-one'. But, like me, she hadn't met 15-year-old Paul Greening.

"The youngest of six children, he became notorious when his drug dealing dad was sentenced to 15 years imprisonment for importing cocaine. He was a nasty little thug who enjoyed belittling, bullying and attacking vulnerable boys and girls. Greening had the ability to spot a long-term victim who would always do what he or she was told.

"It was a posh looking school in a nice area, with trees in the street where houses had front gardens. A world away from the narrow backstreets and terraced houses of East London. But looks can be deceptive, hence the phrase 'never judge a book by its cover'. Gable Brook Comprehensive was a school rife with bullying and sexual abuse.

"I had moved from a concrete jungle to what would become a suburban nightmare. Although days away from my 13th birthday I already had the breasts of a teenager. With my long legs and blonde hair, burly builders were already wolf-whistling and older boys were noticing me. Sadly that is the way of the world, though what happened next isn't and never should be.

"Although looking much older than my years, I was a shy girl who walked with her head down. I'd do anything to avoid eye contact, confrontation or unwanted conversations. I was a normal youngster who was soon to be teenage girl, completely innocent and still a child. That was about to change.

"It's my first morning at Gable Brook Comprehensive. I have a new bag, a uniform I hate and butterflies in my stomach. Girls ignore me as if I'm invisible. Unfortunately, I'm noticed by a group of boys hanging out in the cloakroom. I could feel their eyes boring into me as I walked alone along the corridor, and within seconds I was surrounded by Paul Greening and his gang. No words were exchanged, and without warning the sneering skinhead lifted up my skirt. I froze like a deer in headlights. I could hear the laughter, but to this day have no idea how long my navy blue knickers were on show to a bunch of giggling schoolboys. I felt a hand between my legs and heard the words: 'I'm Paul. Paul Greening. You've probably heard of me. Welcome to Gable Brook.'

"My legs went weak and I felt sick. I then made the biggest mistake of my life and one I'd live to regret: I never reported the assault! I was the new kid in town with no idea who to turn to for help. I had no friends, and knew none of the teachers. It seemed easier to say nothing, and on my first day didn't want the label of 'grass'. I stayed silent, others didn't.

"The Assembly Hall was at the other end of the building and home to 800 students. Where to sit? If I go to the front it's my best chance to make eye contact with a teacher, and offers protection from Greening, who I'd spotted at the back of the hall. He wouldn't be able to touch me, but still had the ability to hurt me. The girls sitting behind laugh so loud, I know they are laughing about me. I can't stop myself. I turn around and see Chrissie Hudson, a gobby girl with the build of a ballet dancer and stare of a heavyweight boxer. Years later we would clash.

"She's surrounded by a group of girls all wearing looks that say 'we know what Paul Greening did to you'. Her eyes meet mine for a split second. 'Slag', she mouths silently before turning away and waving to the grinning skinhead in the back row. I thought to myself 'welcome to Gable Brook Comprehensive'.

"The Headmaster, a local Magistrate with a liberal reputation, hadn't a clue what was going on within the walls of his own school. He had no idea, no neck, a creepy comb-over hairstyle with a mountain of dandruff on his shoulders. I couldn't decide if he'd upset his hairdresser or was morphing into Arthur Scargill. The 80s Union Leader had the worst haircut on the planet, a shredded wheat version of a 'Donald Trump'.

"I quickly decided Gable Brook Comprehensive wasn't the school for me. It was full of bullies, bitchy girls and teachers who didn't seem interested. The next five years would be a nightmare and anything but 'education, education, education'. I somehow made it through the first day without a nuclear meltdown. I survived. I wasn't happy but it gave me hope. Maybe all new girls were treated the same. Was it just a sick form of initiation? If I kept my mouth shut and didn't grass, maybe in time I'd be accepted. I was wrong, very wrong. The bullying, sexual abuse and intimidation would continue for years.

"Paul Greening saw my silence as a sign of weakness, and it gave him the green light to continue. From that day there was no stopping him, and the older I got the worse the abuse. After that incident on my first day at Gable Brook, Greening targeted me on a daily basis and every term the abuse got worse. I was so scared, I'd let him assault me in private and humiliate me in public. He had two elder brothers who controlled the estate, and he ran the school. The scumbag called himself 'the skinhead Reggie Kray', but he was no teenage gangster. Greening was just a bully boy who beat up younger boys and picked on girls. Unfortunately that was me more than most, and after the first week there was no stopping him. In the playground, the classroom, to and from school, over the local park, he was always there and taking more and more liberties. I was powerless to stop him, and he saw me as the perfect victim. An only child with no big brothers to protect me. The new kid in town with no friends. I was his plaything, a non-person with no feelings and no right to a childhood.

"When the abuse started I was 12, innocent and defenceless. He was three years older with a gang to back him up. With hindsight, and as an adult, I can understand why they followed him. At the time I saw him as just a bully. An evil bastard who did what he wanted whenever he felt like it. But Greening was a cunning bastard who used both charm and violence to get what he wanted. A genuine psychopath and narscistic Nazi. He could turn the charm on and off like a tap.

"Though most people feared him, some of his gang actually liked him. He gave them power, easy pickings, access to girls, drugs and protection money from vulnerable students.

"The first time he hit me, he slapped me across the face so hard, I saw tiny stars. I was thirteen. He was 16.

"Paul Greening and his gang got their kicks from hurting people. I spent five years being humiliated and assaulted on an almost daily basis.

"The first time he raped me, I was 14 and it continued on a weekly basis for the next two years. He groomed and controlled me the same way Muslim paedophile gang's targeted underage girls in the North of England.

"Paul Greening is proof that evil perverts come from all ethnic backgrounds. I would be told where and when to turn up. We would meet behind the school sports hall, the back of the park, in empty garages, or worse, his house. This meant his parents would be out so the abuse would last longer.

"It also meant his violent brothers could turn up at any time and he always took great pleasure in freaking me out with that threat."

Taylor talks about her father:

"He was a horrible small-minded and racist bigot. A bully who treated my mum like shit. In many ways he was very similar to Paul Greening. Selfish, arrogant and violent.

"He had one view of the world and it was his. As a child I thought he was `big and powerful` but as an adult I saw him for what he was. A skinny little runt with a lots to say behind closed doors but never had the guts to repeat it in public. From the safety of our lounge, when fuelled by alcohol he`d sing `Hang all the blacks, gas all the Jews and burn all the queers`.

"His other pet hate was Top of the Pops and singers wearing make-up. Boy George and David Bowie would really freak him out.

"My dad was a pathetic armchair General who sorted out the problems of the world wearing Tesco jeans, a string vest and tatty carpet slippers. He was the spitting image of George Roper, the workshy layabout from ITV`s classic comedy George & Mildred. God knows what my mum ever saw him.

"Apart from beer and fags the only true love of his life was Adolf Hitler. The Fuhrer was his political guru and Bernard Manning* was his comic hero

"He would say things like `when I was a kid there were signs in Bed & Breakfast hotels, shops and pubs all over London saying NO dogs, NO Blacks and NO Irish`.They were the good old days.

"He hated all immigrants which is why he moved us out of the East End and why we settled in Stanhope. So in a way it`s his fault that I met Paul Greening.

* Manning was a terrible Northern comedian who was banned from TV for being racist and making vile gags against Blacks, Jews, Women and Gays

"We were never close. He didn't love me and the feeling was mutual. I disliked him because of how he treated my mum and didn't agree with his racist view of the world.

"But I HATED him for moving me out of East London and indirectly delivering me into the clutches of Paul Greening

"I am many things. I'm a self-confessed serial killer. I am proud of that fact. But I am not a hypocrite, which is why I never attended his funeral never visited his grave."

FOUR

The Summer of 2015

In the summer of 2015, Taylor swaps the feelings of depression for those of anger. She is haunted by devastating memories from her childhood. Her sweet dreams are replaced by recurring nightmares. Awake or asleep, she can't escape seeing the face of Paul Greening. He's always been lurking in the back of her mind, but now he's at the forefront.

"I think it's some kind of psychiatric disorder when you have more than one personality, or hear multiple voices in your head. That is what it felt like when I tried to sleep. I'd hear voices reminding me of the past, and others chastising me for not getting revenge.

"I just wanted to forget, amnesia would be nice - I just couldn't clear my mind. Did he rape my head, too?

"I knew I couldn't contain my anger forever"

It was reports of historical sex crimes committed by 70s celebrities like Sir Jimmy Saville, Gary Glitter and Rolf Harris that re-ignited Taylor's nightmares. They would lead to her going on a killing spree that would shock the world. In just over a month, she tortured and murdered eight men, and was only caught after confessing to a tabloid journalist.

"I always wanted revenge, but convinced myself I'd left it too late and that they'd got away with it. I genuinely believed they'd escaped justice. Then everything changed.

"Famous men, household names I'd grown up watching on TV, were being arrested and sent to prison for historical sex crimes. I was witnessing it being reported daily on TV and avidly reading reports in newspapers."

It was the publicity surrounding historical sex crimes and Operation Yewtree that inspired Taylor Shelley to seek justice. Though instead of picking up the phone to the police she picked up a knife and became a serial killer. These were the stories on SKY News and on the front page of every tabloid.

SIR JIMMY SAVILE: a close friend of Maggie Thatcher and fundraiser for the Tory party was exposed as a paedophile. He was knighted in 1990 and had been a child abuser for 60 years.

In 1978 punk legend Johnny Rotten spoke out during a Radio One interview. He revealed that everyone at Top of the Pops and the BBC knew Saville was to quote The Sex Pistol "a kiddie fiddler`. The Authorities took no action and Johnny Rotten/Lydon was banned by Radio One. The interview was not broadcast.

But last year on ITV, John Lydon was interviewed by Piers Morgan, he retold the story and Piers played the interview from 1978. So far 63 girls have come forward and 34 rapes have been reported.

GARY GLITTER: The glam rocker was imprisoned for possession of child pornography in 1999, and child sex abuse and attempted rape in 2006 and 2015. In November 2005 Glitter was arrested in Ho Chi Minh City Vietnam, while trying to board a flight to Thailand. 6 Vietnamese girls, aged from 11 to 23 claimed Glitter had had sex with them. He is currently serving a 16 year sentence.

ROLF HARRIS: The veteran entertainer was jailed on 12 counts of indecent assault that took place between 1968 and 1998, on 4 female victims, then aged 8 to 19. He was stripped of his OBE and MBE and sentenced to 5 years and 9 months in prison.

MAX CLIFFORD: Publicist to the stars Max Clifford is also a convicted sex offender. He was found guilty of eight indecent assaults on girls aged 14 to 19. He was sentenced to 8 years.

FRED TALBOT: ITV weatherman, was sentenced to 5 years for sexually assaulting 2 schoolboys.

STUART HALL: BBC broadcaster, was convicted on 15 counts of Indecent assault.

OPERATION YEWTREE:*
Operation Yewtree was a Scotland Yard investigation into historical sex crimes. It was set up in the wake of the Jimmy Saville revelations.
Detectives are currently looking into historical sex crimes committed by un-named politicians, celebrities and leading figures in the British Establishment.
The late Liberal MP Cyril Smith has been publically named as an abuser of young boys. It was the publicity surrounding these historical sex crimes that contributed to the thoughts in Taylor Shelley's mind, urging her to seek revenge and ultimately turning Taylor Shelly into a serial killer.

*The latest scandal that broke just before Christmas 2016 is that football coaches at clubs all over the UK have been accused of assaulting young boys. Former players have come forward and some coaches have already been sent to prison.

"The voices in my head were asking questions. Firstly, 'why didn't you speak out at the time?' This made me feel weak and ashamed. Like the victims of the well-known abusers, I hadn't spoken out either at the time. I understood the victims, but then, what good is speaking out so long after the horrific abuse occurred?

"Then, 'what are you going to do about it now?' I felt angrier than at any other time in my life and something just clicked in my brain. Speaking out was not enough. I can't explain, but violent thoughts took over my mind, and voices were telling me to do something about it. Do something to every single one of them. Getting revenge on them all would mean I would become a serial killer. I turned it over in my mind. Did I care? No, if that was what they would call me for doing what I had to do, then so be it. I would become a serial killer. It sounded so unladylike."

Before deciding on this extreme cure and alternative form of medication, Taylor tried many solutions. Everything from fast drugs to Yoga. Nothing worked. She was an angry young women who slept with black men to get back at her racist father, and had lesbian flings because she hated men.

After fleeing her home town in fear of Paul Greening, she became a nomad, travelling all over the UK and Europe attending music festivals.

"I was always a massive Jam fan and obsessed with Paul Weller, so I followed The Style Council everywhere. I could forget my troubles listening to songs like *When the Walls Come Tumbling Down*, *Speak Like A Child* and *My Ever Changing Moods*.

"I lived on a diet of little blue pills, white powder, Vodka, Red Bull and Veggie Burgers.

"My dad hated my lifestyle and dress sense, so the more he complained, the shorter my skirts got and the darker my boyfriends.

"I spent my teens and early 20s hanging out at Mod clubs like the Ilford Palais, Sneakers in West London, and Soho coffee bars.

"It was a great time to be young, as barriers were coming down in society. Attitudes to homosexuality, divorce, race, drugs, were all changing for the better. I was happy to embrace the modern world.

"Although a self-confessed party animal, I also had a strong social conscience and was to the left of Tony Benn. I was a regular at Rock Against Racism gigs and Red Wedge Concerts."

At thirty, after following The Stone Roses, indulging in Rave culture and embracing the Brit pop scene, she settled down in Southend-on-Sea. Her hairdressing salon became a chain of three, the money was rolling in, but she wasn't truly happy.

A ten-year relationship with a common law partner fizzled out, an on-off romance with hard-core gangster Harry Harris gave her excitement, but she couldn't shake off her troubled past.

"When I first met Danny, my partner, my common-law husband of ten years, I kept a big secret: the story of my childhood sexual abuse. He never knew nothing about my past. I loved him to bits, but the ghost/shadow of Paul Greening was always on my mind. It came between us and eventually led to us splitting up.

"Danny knew I'd been promiscuous, but so had he. We shared a love of fast drugs, but I couldn't share my past with him. We rowed. I cheated. He was a lovely bloke and in many ways I was the perfect partner. I trusted him one hundred per cent, but I could never trust myself. I didn't trust life. I always thought that when things were going well something or someone would spoil everything.

"I could never fully accept that he truly loved me. After all he was a man, and men had always hurt me. Either by doing things against my will or when I let them get close. So as a form of protection, I always walked away from a relationship. I was always the one to leave. I left Danny, who was a kind, peaceful and chilled out guy with the personality of a new age hippy who dressed like a Mod, for Harry Harris.

"Harry Harris was an East End gangster who was dangerous and thrived on violence. Harry had shot and stabbed people and his violent reputation in East London was legendary. He got high on physical combat but I just knew, from the minute we met, he would never hurt me. I felt safe in his arms, in his company, in his bed.

"Harry was ten years younger than me and I'd never been so attracted to anyone in my life. Maybe subconsciously and without realising it at the time, I knew he would be the man to help me take down Paul Greening."

The media coverage of multiple arrests of famous celebrities for historical sex crimes gave Taylor the idea of how she would finally get peace of mind. The dedicated follower of fashion became a serial killer.

FIVE

Times Change

In the early 1980s, Paul Greening was a bully-boy thug who ruled the West Ham Estate in the Essex town of Stanhope. Over the years, he had acquired vast wealth, political power and respectability.

"When I saw pictures of him wearing a Tory rosette and posing with famous politicians the anger kicked in. I knew I had to destroy him. After suffering in silence for 30 years, I got to the point where I couldn't stay silent any longer. It was too late to speak out, but not to hit out"

Unlike Taylor, the Tory MP doesn't dwell on, or even think about, the past. He's forgotten about the hell he put her through. That is all about to change.

Although now a successful and confident woman, Taylor Shelley has never forgotten the bullied teenager she once was. She survived against the odds and today all of the power is in her hands. They say revenge is a dish best served cold but Taylor wants it to be cold blooded. She wants Old Testament justice.

Confucius said:
"Before embarking upon revenge dig two graves"

Taylor planned to dig three. Permanent retirement homes for Paul Greening, his sidekick John Hunter and a third for the bad horrific memories of her teenage past. Despite Brexit, the death of David Bowie and the election of Donald Trump. The world moves on and circumstances change. Taylor was now judge, Jury and Executioner. She would personally carry out death sentences on Paul Greening and his co-defendants.

"They called me a slag, slut, a whore, but never a victim or by my name. They never saw me as a innocent victim or as Taylor Shelley. I wasn't good enough for a name. That would make me a real person with feelings. My pet name/nickname was Tonka. Tonka Taylor. Or as they would sneer `Bonka Tonka`. By calling me Tonka Taylor or Bonka Tonka it was as if they didn't have to think of me as a real person. Their sisters and girlfriends had names. They were called Debbie, Anna, Sharon. I wasn't worthy of such respect.

"They didn't want to think of me of being just like them. Another teenage girl who just wanted to have fun and be happy. I just wanted a fucking life. A normal childhood. Schooldays are meant to be the best days of your life. Full of happy memories, achievements and good times. Most people can look back fondly at what they call `the good old days`. I can't.

"Paul Greening stole my childhood. Him and his friends destroyed my teenage years. The time has come to wipe them out!"

Sitting in her Essex Hairdressing salon, Taylor once again finds her past unravelling, but this time she has a solution. She will soon confront her demons and slay all of her dragons.

Amid the whirling hairdryers and snipping scissors, she starts to wonder how she can achieve this dream. Taylor has already tracked down Paul Greening MP, thanks to his love of self-publicity and high-profile career. She will use Facebook and the Electoral Roll to locate the rest of the gang. Her plan is to kill as many as possible, as quickly as she can, to avoid detection.

Greening is different, as she wants his death to involve torture and long hours of drawn out suffering. Ultimate pain and humiliation.

How can she put this plan into action? The obvious answer is to recruit long-time lover Harry Harris. He is the perfect choice. A leading authority in the profession of violence. The East End gangster is also infatuated with the stunning Cougar and will do anything to make her happy.

SIX

The Cockney Capone

Say 'hello' to Harry Harris, the Cockney Capone, the modern day gangster with old school morals.

"Various newspapers have called him the 'Dillinger of Dagenham' or the 'Capone of Canning Town'. I just call him Harry"

He is her best friend with benefits, and has been her on/off lover for many years. Harry Harris is a career criminal who grew up reading about the underworld exploits of Reg & Ronnie Kray and the adventures of The Great Train Robbers - hero-worshipping Freddie Foreman and watching classic British gangster films like Get Carter, Villain, Performance and The Long Good Friday. Fact or fiction, it didn't bother him as he also liked Robin Hood, Jesse James, Guy Fawkes and Dick Turpin.

Maybe because of his Irish heritage, he always supported the underdog and was attracted to rebels like Georgie Best and Hurricane Higgins. Harry had a lifelong hatred of perverts and paedophiles like Paul Greening.

He was too young to be a skinhead, but it was the teenage cult that fired his passion for mindless violence and casual sex. The future gangster spent his youth hanging out with older boys, 'learning his trade', watching and understanding how to create an image and build a reputation for violence.

The 15-year-old boy with a man's body supplemented his youthful energy with vast amounts of amphetamine, steroids and cans of coke.

He didn't carry a government health warning, but he was an explosion waiting to happen – a ticking bomb with a killer punch.

Today the teenage thug is a 35-year-old 'face' on the manor, with a loyal gang and code of honour. They live by the motto 'what goes round comes around'.

Harry's gang include some of the hardest men in East London with more convictions for violence then the combined total of the notorious ICF.

HARRYS GANG:
Warwick Courtney, Wayne Jackson, Dodgy Dave Diamond, Turbo and Mad Martin Smith.

Harry believes in loyalty and is always nice to his mum, little old ladies and young children. He is a Cockney Capone with a heart of gold and a stare that can kill. Harry Harris is the reason Tory MP Paul Greening is a dead man walking.

Taylor will personally kill the pervert and strike the final and fatal blows, but without her boyfriend's help it won't be half as much fun. Unlike the others, this would be much more than just another murder. It would be bloody, dramatic and chilling - like a real-life horror movie - more of an honour killing, involving torture, humiliation and closure.

Most women who've experienced sexual abuse or domestic violence will applaud the slaughter of a serial sex offender. You wouldn't be human if you didn't laugh at his plight or enjoy his final moments.

First he loses his liberty, then his dignity, and then his life. But who cares? It's payback time. Greening is about to pay the ultimate price for stealing the childhood of Taylor Shelley. Read on and I guarantee you will enjoy the total humiliation and extermination of a swaggering bully.

Taylor Shelley will kill the first seven on her own, but the murder of Tory MP Paul Greening has to be special. An event. A Show Trial. So she turns to East End gangster boyfriend Harry Harris for help.

Taylor picks her moment. The timing is perfect. They have just had sex and Harry is 'Charlied up' to the eyeballs. He is putty in her hands and cant resist. The fact she is naked means he has no resistance to her requests. Harry is so much under her spell she could convince him that there is life on Mars.

Lighting a large spliff and taking a deep breath she tells him all about her past. The words run out of her mouth like a stream – never stopping, emotionless and cold. Harry listens, straining to keep his emotions harnessed, afraid to stop her and at the same time loathing what he was hearing and longing to hush her flow of bad memoires.

The veins in his neck were standing to attention, his eyes bulging out of their sockets. If looks could kill Paul Greening would already be dead. Taylor had seen him 'lose his rag' a hundred times but this was different. Another level. This was personal.

As the words ended Taylor closed her mouth and breathed heavily through her nose as if to compose herself. She had learned in yoga to take a cleansing breath – as if that would solve the problems – maybe for some, never for her. Harry pulled on his boxers, chopped out another line of Charlie.

"You have my word the pervert is dead. The bastard better have good security because he is in for a world of pain"

Harry is more Reggie Kray than Sun Agony Aunt Deirdre Saunders. He is sympathetic, but from his background doesn't know how to show his feelings. He can show rage. He knows how to do that very well indeed. But sympathy and love are not in his reportoire. This is a alien situation for a East End gangster. Harry feels violent rage. He see's himself as the modern day white knight. He will rescue the damsel in distress.

"I am not fucking happy. I'm fucking raging, angrier then I've ever been. I didn't know you then, never met the bastard, but I soon will. I cant wait to introduce myself and I wont be shaking hands, I`ll be blowing his fucking balls off. Believe me this is personal." Harry said snarling as he spoke.

"I don't want you getting into trouble for something that happened 30 years ago. I didn't tell you for that. I don't want you to kill him just to snatch him for me, I`ll do the rest." Taylor said.

"If that`s what you want, consider me hired. I`m just the man for the job. The scumbag needs to learn a lesson. I`m gonna help you fuck up his life." Harry added, feeling much calmer now he had decided what needed to be done.

"I`m gonna end his life." Taylor said quietly.

"It`s a situation that needs fixing. I cant wait to introduce myself to him" Harry added.

Twenty-four hours later Greening would be kidnapped thrown into the back of a van and taken on his last ever car journey.

SEVEN

Stanhope

The small town buzzed with the story of mass murders. Seven men have been murdered, each stabbed to death within a one mile radius. The authorities were baffled, were they killed at random or targeted for a reason?

The police appeared to be stunned and bemused, devoting their efforts to minute forensic examinations of the crime scenes. Why on earth, they pondered, would anybody want to execute seven local men?

A murder detective told a journalist on the Essex Echo 'There's all sorts of possibilities, and at the moment most of them are unprovable. We have forensics' covering every inch of the scene, but nothing interesting has been found yet. We will keep looking as it's all there is to go on. People don't just kill people at random in Stanhope. At the end of the day it'll be all down to motive and finding the murder weapon. Find that, and we'll find the killer.'

Talk about stating the bleeding obvious.

There hadn't been a major crime or murder in Stanhope since 1980, the year West Ham won the FA Cup and The Jam were topping the charts.

Local journalist Kelly Baxter was after a scoop that could change her life. The ambitious hack was bored of writing stories about traffic casualties, alcohol-related violence and jumble sales.

Kelly was just the kind of hungry young reporter that tabloid editors love. Female, attractive, intelligent, a workaholic, with no interest in having babies.

She had the writing skills of Julie Burchill, the work ethic of David Bowie and the sleep pattern of Maggie Thatcher.

There was a massive murder investigation taking place on her patch, and like any ambitious and talented cub reporter, she wanted to be part of it.

Kelly Baxter wanted to make her name and follow in the footsteps of legends like Sue Reid, Jane Moore and current tabloid queen Rebekah Woods.

At first it seemed as if the victims had nothing in common apart from all being local, white and aged 50. But after murders number 2, 3 and 4, a bizarre link to each homicide is discovered. Essex police had their first clue. The same photograph has been found near each of the dead bodies. Close enough to be found, but not as close as to be included in the forensic scene of the crime search area. The murderer had cleverly hidden the photo and it was only found by mistake in a waste area near body number 3. It was almost tossed away as irrelevant, hadn't it been for one young officer recognising one of the victims.

Crime scene exhibits from the first murder are revisited, and revealed a copy of the same photograph close by. A picture of the 1982 Stanhope Boys under 16 Football Team. Why was the killer leaving a calling card?

Now that a link was emerging - a bizarre pattern, detectives decided everyone in the picture was in danger. Seven were already dead but what of the other five?

The sleepy town of Stanhope was now a hotbed of activity and virtually under siege. It was like a full-blown invasion. The streets were full of murder squad detectives searching for bodies, Fleet Street hacks digging for dirt, and local newshound Kelly Baxter looking for a scoop - a story that could lead to her dream job: a picture by-line column on a Fleet Street tabloid.

Mass murder, like a Royal Wedding, sells newspapers - so for day after day, the killings are splashed across the front pages of The Sun, Mirror and Daily Mail.

The multiple slayings also led the 24-hour news bulletins on the BBC, ITV and Sky. But who would be first to expose the violent and perverted past of Paul Greening, the Conservative politician with many enemies? A selfish, dishonest, devious, lecherous, sadistic, self-serving, ultra-right-wing MP.

Greening became a Member of Parliament by marrying the daughter of multi-millionaire banker Sir Roderick Pratt-Dawson, who controlled his local Tory party.

The solicitor Camilla Pratt-Dawson had no connection with Stanhope and wasn't even an Essex Girl. Her family had always lived in Oxfordshire, and the 'odd couple' met during a hedonistic holiday in Ibiza. Camilla wasn't his type, not even her own mother would call her attractive. She wasn't slim, blonde or good-looking, but Greening was attracted by her plummy accent, double-barrelled name and bank account. Camilla looked like a man in drag, but was his passport to the good life.

They married within a year of him taking her virginity, and Greening moved to the Shires. She was perfect for him and his ruthless ambition to climb the greasy pole. Over the years he quickly changed from Essex wide boy to an assured businessman, gradually losing his Cockney accent and good looks. The more ordinary he became in appearance, the more successful he became in business.

As his father-in-law rose through the ranks of the Conservative Party so did Greening. First as a local councillor, then as a parliamentary candidate, before becoming the Tory MP for Oxford Marshes. When first elected, he still had his good looks and full head of hair. With his flashy suits and Boris Johnson soundbites he was good copy.

He fast became a media darling, appearing on TV shows like Have I Got News For You, The Last Leg and ironically Would I Lie To You.

Paul Greening played the game like it had never been played before, making nasty, cutting comments about his political rivals to camera, with barely disguised glee.

The new MP, with his love of publicity, became known in Fleet Street as 'dial-a-quote'.

He irritated people so much that even Grandees in his own party started to declare their dislike of him.

When he wasn't being controversial on TV, he took to Twitter to spew his outrageous hate-filled tweets. Did President Trump model himself on the right-wing Tory politician?

Greening was proof you don't have to be particularly clever or educated to get your big break. You just have to marry into the British establishment. It also helps if you have a cold heart, a sinister streak and a dark side.

Greening managed to make a very good life for himself. Political pundits predicted promotion to the Cabinet, some even tipping him as a future Prime Minister. But, like his wife, father-in-law and voters, they knew nothing about his sordid past as a serial rapist. They soon would.

It would be the end of his political career, and his life as a Z list celebrity would be over. No more holiday snaps or family gatherings featured in the glossy pages of Hello, OK and Closer. In a perfect world, he would be sharing prison food with the likes of Rolf Harris, Max Clifford and Gary Glitter. But only if the police got to him before Taylor Shelley.

The incident room was a buzz of activity. Pictures of the 7 victims were pinned up on a board, alongside the Stanhope under 16 Football Team of 1982.

Essex police held a News Conference revealing all but one of the missing footballers in the photograph had been found safe and well.

There was no sign of Paul Greening. Was the Tory MP dead or alive? The police were baffled. Why had seven men with no criminal records, apart from parking tickets and speeding points, been brutally butchered in a sleepy suburban town? Stanhope was not New York City, it wasn't even the East End of London.

Inquiries revealed those found dead or alive had one other thing in common - all had attended Gable Brook Comprehensive. But what did that 30-year old photograph have to do with the murders? What was the missing link?

Essex police had no idea the connection was female or Taylor Shelley. They knew they had a serial killer on their hands and as usual their psychologists profiled the serial killer as a young male with a history of violence. Most serial killers are psychopaths. And because psychopaths are born, not made, they would have started their actions at a young age, starting with people and animals they deemed lesser than themselves. They would often torture and kill animals, be cruel to elderly and children before they start their killing spree. Essex police were sure this was the person they were looking for. Psychopathy is passed on from the father to the make child. For a female to be a psychopath, the gene must be present in both the mother and the father. So rare was this that only on very few occasions has the world seen a female psychopathic killer. The thought never crossed the mind of anyone at Essex police – and they would regret that very soon.

Taylor was waiting for her revenge – she could almost taste it. Greening was the first boy to see her naked, to take her virginity, but they were anything but childhood sweethearts. The truth is, he made her life hell. It was a one-sided relationship that lived on in her mind and left a scar on her heart forever. They shared a teenage past. Long forgotten memories for him and unhappy ones her.

If Harry Harris was cut from the same cloth as Reggie Kray, then Greening was from the same mould as Mr Blobby. A tub of lard who got off on bullying women and raping teenage girls. Harris is one of the chaps, a hardcore gangster and Greening is about to became his next victim. The Cockney Capone is addicted to cocaine and infatuated with Taylor. She uses this obsession to her advantage. The gung-ho gangster wants to blow the pervert's head off, but she convinces him to do it her way.

Fifty miles away in his safe suburban home, Tory MP Paul Greening is unaware that his perverted past is about to catch up with him.

It will soon be his turn to be scared, used, abused and then executed.

Now, Thirty years on, Taylor is about to get justice. A six year campaign of terror cannot go unpunished any longer.

Revenge is long overdue. The time has come to get even.

EIGHT

Friends Reunited

The peace of the sleepy seaside town is rudely shattered when 7 dead bodies are found within a month. Local police have no idea just who is committing these seemingly motiveless crimes.

"I am a great talker and must have spoken a million words in my lifetime, but none sounded sweeter than the few I said when I was reunited with Paul Greening. When I walked into the room, he was naked and trussed up like a turkey. It was reconciliation on my terms, and he looked exactly what he was, a pathetic creature. It was his turn to be a victim. One of his guards was Warwick Courtney, a massive black guy who looked like Mike Tyson."

This was important and symbolic, as Greening was a life-long racist. A fascist bovver boy who grew up to be a right-wing Tory politician.

"He had no idea what was happening and was quite rightly terrified and looked so different from the last time I had seen him. His hair had long disappeared, as had the square jaw and muscular physique, now buried under a mountain of flab".

Time had not been kind to the bloated bully and teenage sex offender. Taylor, on the other hand, had blossomed from a schoolgirl stunner into a beautiful woman. Her feline face, with its high cheekbones and come-to-bed eyes, was framed by hair tinted strawberry blonde. In middle-age, she still turned heads as a dead ringer for Britain's Got Talent Judge Amanda Holden. She took a deep breath and went inside to face the man she had hated for 30 years.

"I just stared at the fat, bald, pathetic man trembling in front of me, and asked myself 'why was I ever scared of that bastard?'."

***

She spoke in a very quiet, level voice, as one might speak to a young child who had been naughty.

"Hello Paul, it's lovely to meet you" she said sarcastically.

There was no response.

"What's up? Don't you recognize me with my clothes on? Taylor Shelley. Or Tonka Taylor as you called me. The young girl you treated like shit. The teenage girl you raped and terrorised

"I won't waste any time asking how you've been, because I know, and I don't much care. I'm sure you care even less about me, but you'd have to be really thick not to know what I think about you. You'd also have to have no memory"

Unfortunately for Greening, she had a very good memory, going right back to her very first day at Gable Brook Comprehensive.

"Think of this as a citizen's arrest with you on trial in a Kangaroo Court. This time you're the helpless victim. You have no human rights, no legal representation, and guess what? I've already found you guilty."

The combined powers of Jesus Christ, the Queen, Superman, the Pope, the Prime Minister, James Bond and Saint Christopher could not save the Tory MP.

"You'd have to be stupid, which I know you're not, not to work out what I want.

The death penalty."

Greening wobbled like a jelly as the colour drained from his fat face.

"I don't just want revenge, I want you dead - and believe me, very soon you will be." She wasn't joking, but he didn't know that.

Taylor felt a surge of adrenaline fire through her body and remembered why she became a serial killer. It had nothing to do with excitement or blood lust - it was all about revenge, pure and simple.

They say revenge is a dish best served cold, but Taylor wants it to be cold-blooded. She's had enough of the years of mental torture and wants Old Testament style justice for the sexual abuse suffered in the past.

Greening was starting to sweat. He was both whimpering and crying at the same time, shaking his head, spraying sweat, wriggling his cuffed wrists like a puppy dog with a new toy. It was a bad case of the shakes.

***

"Greening was no longer a tough guy or a bully, but a broken man falling to pieces in front of my eyes. His skin was turning grey, he was sobbing and looking older by the second"

Taylor felt no pity for her former tormentor. Just massive feelings of elation, satisfaction and, more than anything, power. This was her moment - and like a fanatical dictator she was in complete control. It was her decision and hers alone how much longer Greening had to live. Like a US President it was her finger on the button. She had the final say. As a 12-year-old, Taylor had been assaulted by this pervert and then raped as a Teenager.

"I've only truly hated one person in my life, and that is him. My blood was starting to boil. The roles were now reversed and for the first time in my life I had him at my mercy. It was my road to Damascus moment, my landing on the moon, my number one record. I was close to getting closure. His evil stare was burnt into my soul and had burned for decades. The fire was about to be put out. He now had a big fat white pasty face, the eyes had lost their menace and his stare did not scare me anymore. He was a bloated, overweight middle-aged man and I was no longer a terrified teenager. I'd already found the courage to kill seven times, and he was about to become victim number eight. I saw the fear in his eyes. I felt happy and wanted to celebrate but first I had a job to do. The execution of a sex offender.

"The initial plan was to give him a drink laced with the rape drug Rohypnol, then beat him to death with a baseball bat. I wanted it over and done with as quickly as possible because I thought I'd still be in awe of him. But I didn't feel scared anymore. I had done the others on my own, and they were all rushed because I didn't want to be caught.

"Most were committed in public, this time it would be a private execution and I had help. Greening was a broken man. I could take my time and enjoy his final moments. I could humiliate and torture the bastard before putting him to sleep. When I told him I was going to tattoo the word 'rapist' on his penis prison style with a bottle of ink, he almost passed out."

NINE

The Death Penalty

Why did Paul Greening deserve to die and what were his major crimes? Rape, Gang Rape, Sexual Assault, Grooming, Bullying, Intimidation, Stealing A Childhood.

"There were so many incidents, too many to recall but some stand out more than most. The three gang rapes were the worst, but I never forgot the years of humiliation. The embarrassment of being stripped naked in a room full of grinning teenage boys. The hatred of myself for allowing Paul Greening to control my youth. Some boys go too far. Some boys will break your heart. But one boy can ruin your life.

"I used to pray every day, even though I'm not religious, that one day Greening would pay for his crimes. I'd lie in bed, and stare up at the ceiling, thinking if there is a God he'll make sure I get justice.

"Certain incidents have never left me. The first time the gang stripped me naked at the back of the local park and Greening took my virginity.

"The day I was taken to an empty house and gang raped.

"The time they removed all my clothes during a train journey to Southend-On-Sea.

"In those days, British Rail trains were single compartments so you couldn't see what was going on. Me and a girl called Janice Lamb had boarded the train for a nice day out at the seaside. Neither of us knew we'd been spotted by Greening on our way to the station. We soon found out. As the train pulled away, Greening and his gang ran along the platform and jumped into the carriage. Janice and I were both prisoners, but as usual I was the main target. The journey lasted only 10 minutes but that was long enough for me to be humiliated and embarrassed.

"Greening and John Hunter grabbed and undressed me in front of my friend and the rest of the gang. I'd been stripped many times, but this was the first time in front of another female. It was a hot and sunny day so I was only wearing a T-shirt and skirt, which took them seconds to remove. My underwear quickly followed. Although their hands were grabbing and groping, it had nothing to do with sex. It was all about humiliating me in front of another girl.

"The train pulled into Benfleet station and I begged to be given my clothes back. I was terrified of a member of staff or an adult seeing what was going on and calling the police. No way did I want my parents finding out.

"Greening found my begging and pleading hilarious. He eventually returned my skirt and top, but not my underwear. The rest of the gang found it hysterical when the bastard threw my bra and pants out of the window.

"Such was my mind-set and fear of Greening, I spent the next few hours walking round Southend-On-Sea with no nickers.

"Luckily my skirt was just about long enough to cover my bottom. It was humiliating and scary as every time we walked past a pub or seafront café he would threaten to pull up my skirt. As always with Greening, it was always more about power and control then sex. He threatened to rip my skirt off unless I shoplifted from Woolworths, or sung and danced in McDonalds.

"The more he showed off, the more his mates laughed. Why didn't I scream, run away or ask for help? It was a combination of fear and what psychiatrists call the `Stockholm Syndrome`. A state of mind where a victim willingly co-operates with his or her attackers - one of the most famous examples of this being when kidnapped heiress Patty Hearst fell in love with one of her abductors. The privileged posh girl became a bank robber.

Greening would press his face against mine and say 'I can smell the fear dripping off you'. Adding 'you will always do what I want'.

"The train journey home was going to be worse, as I knew what was going to happen. All afternoon he'd bragged 'I'm fucking her on the way back'. I couldn't stop that from happening, but as daft at it sounds today, my main fear wasn't being raped but praying nobody would be watching. He'd already raped me in front of his gang, which was humiliating enough, but raping me in front of my friend would be unbearable.

"I wasn't happy, but relieved when just the two of us got into the empty compartment. As soon as the train pulled out of the station, he pinned me down and had his 30 seconds of fun. What happened next confirmed that Greening was always more interested in control then sex. He was what most women would call a lousy lover, who suffered with premature ejaculation. The perverted rapist was only happy when bullying.

"My friend was in another compartment with the rest of the gang and they decided to try it on. But Janice wasn't me, and although scared, she fought back. As they pulled at her clothes she shouted, screamed and kicked out.

"When the train stopped at Stanhope, gang warfare almost broke out. A grinning Greening bragged about 'shagging me', as he put it, then John Hunter revealed they'd tried to strip Janice. Greening was not happy. If looks could kill, Hunter would be dead. He wasn't angry because he had sympathy for Janice, but because Hunter had acted without his permission. Greening was the leader of the gang and felt he'd been disrespected.

"What happened next confirmed the hold he had over the gang, me, and soon Janice. Paul Greening, because of his older brothers and army of cousins, was unstoppable and untouchable. No-one dared stand up to him. Such was his fearsome reputation, the Nazi loving skinhead had two non-white boys in his gang. I could never understand why the West Indian Paul Bishop and mixed-race Casey Newton were in his gang. What was the attraction? The perks that came from being in the gang or the protection it gave them? Was it safer to have him as a mate rather than an enemy?

"He mocked the gang, saying, 'So you couldn't get all her clothes off' adding 'I don't ask, I tell people what to do'.

"I remember looking at Janice and thinking 'run off while you can'. She didn't, and we all found ourselves walking towards the secluded sea wall area of Stanhope. Like me, the rest of the gang knew why, and what was going to happen. Greening was going to prove a point and remind the gang who was leader.

"Stanhope station to the sea wall was a fifteen minute walk down Fairview Chase, Wharf Road and then along a dirt track to a clearing in the bushes. It was also home to the gang's hideout, a Second World War air raid shelter. A perfect place for them to drink beer, take drugs and bring girls. Isolated and secure, they could look out but nobody could see in.

"It was early evening as Greening ushered myself and Janice into the building. There were no lights but it wasn't dark, as holes were cut into the concrete. Greening was back in charge and calling the shots. I wasn't sure what would happen next but knew it would benefit his reputation.

"As the gang waited outside Janice and I were told to take off our tops. I obeyed, she didn't. We were told to take off our skirts. Again I obeyed and she didn't.

"Greening was not amused, and told Janice to 'strip or else' and again she ignored him. I admired her courage but knew it would end in tears.

"Like me, Janice looked much older than 15, had long legs and the biggest breasts in our year. Unlike me, she had never before been targeted by Greening and his gang. She'd witnessed some of the humiliating things he'd done to me in public, but not what went on in private. That was all about to change.

"Greening could not lose face, so as always turned the situation to his advantage, calling in the rest of the gang and saying 'come on, we'll all strip the slags'.

"In their eyes it made him look good. He was sharing the spoils with his mates. To them, he was the big gang leader letting his followers get involved in the fun.

"Within minutes we were both naked, and my friend was close to tears as Greening, Hunter, Bishop and Brown grabbed and groped her. The bully boy was enjoying the power and saying things to impress like 'now then boys, we've got 2 fucking slags to play with'. But Greening was much more of a sick psycho then a traditional rapist. He was a pervert with a split personality and more interest in mental torture than sex.

"Without warning, and as if something clicked in his head, he suddenly changed. He ordered the gang to back off, to stop grabbing and groping and told Janice and me to get dressed. Greening didn't get his kicks from sex but from humiliating and embarrassing his victims. That was mission accomplished. He'd also made himself look big and powerful in front of his mates.

"With Janice naked, I was given the job of calming her down and making sure she didn't talk. On Greening's orders I told her to keep her mouth shout, saying I'd deny everything and that it would be her word against ours. I convinced Janice to stay silent, but lost a friend as she never spoke to me again. Whenever I watch Hollyoaks I think of her as she looked so much like the Mercedes McQueen character.

"That incident proved beyond doubt that Greening was all about power rather than sex. He was more of a sadist then a rapist who got turned on by humiliating me at every opportunity. In his sick and twisted mind, because I never reported that first assault I wasn't a genuine victim. It was as if I'd given him permission to do whatever he wanted, whenever he liked.

"I told Rebekah I didn't want to relive all the rapes, as there were far too many. I believed that revealing his sadistic tendency best portrayed his evil character. The first and final gang rape were the main reasons I became a killer, but it was the years of humiliation, and theft of my childhood that turned me into a serial killer."

The police reports list the incidents taken down when Taylor was interviewed. These included the following:

1) She was stopped on her way to the School Tuck Shop and taken to the empty Annex Building where she was stripped and shut in a cupboard. She was trapped for ten minutes and when let out, to find half the class were waiting to watch as she ran naked along the corridor to retrieve her clothes.

2) She was swimming at the local Lido when Greening, Hunter and Bishop jumped in, surrounded her and in front of a crowded swimming pool pulled off her bikini top and bottom.

3) Her skirt was pulled off at a Youth Club Disco and she then spent an hour hiding in the girls toilet, waiting for Greening to return it.

4) She was dragged into the boys' changing rooms and stripped on Greening's last day at school.

"At various times over the years I was undressed in various classrooms, at the back of school buildings, behind the Youth Club and at different houses. I was only 14 the first time Greening raped me.

"One Sunday evening, the gang spotted me and stopped me from walking out of the local park. I don't know why I didn't scream or shout for help as they surrounded and dragged me into the bushes behind the play area.

"I was a virgin and being raped didn't even occur to me. I just expected to be undressed, embarrassed and humiliated like all previous occasions. By now the gang had stripped me so many times I was almost conditioned to accept it. But this was to be far worse then anything that had happened before.

"I was wearing a navy cardigan and a light blue dress buttoned all down the front. Greening started to undo the buttons and I was pushed to the ground. I put up a token struggle and was soon completely naked. He climbed on top and I could soon feel something between my legs. Greening was raping me. The rest were watching and I could hear them laughing, jeering and arguing who was next.

"I was saved by a passing couple out walking their dog who chased the boys away. The lady helped me to dress but I ran away before they could call the police. Greening was waiting for me at the end of my street. He warned me that if I said a word to anyone, there would be a next time with all the members of the gang. I swore I wouldn't tell a soul, and didn't.

"It was stomach churning and so embarrassing having to face them all in school the next day. I spent all my energy trying to avoid them. Whenever they saw me they would mock, make horrible gestures and smirk. I wanted two things more than anything. I didn't want anyone finding out what happened at the back of Stanhope Park, and didn't want it to happen again. But there soon was another time, another place, but with the same script.

"A few weeks later I was stopped by Chrissie Hudson on my way to school, who informed me 'Paul Greening wants you to bunk off with him. I'm bunking off with Peter Brown at his place'. I wasn't happy, but had no choice, as I'd learned never to disobey any of his orders.

"Chrissie assured me it would just be her boyfriend Peter Brown and Greening waiting at the house. I had no reason to doubt her and no idea what awaited me.

"Brown opened the front door and we both followed him into the hallway and up the stairs. Paul Greening was waiting on the landing. He said nothing and ushered me into the back bedroom. He, Brown and Chrissie Hudson followed

"I wanted to die when I saw, hiding behind the door, were the rest of the gang. Greening pushed me forward and within minutes I was naked and pushed onto the bed.

"As soon as Chrissie and Brown left the room the first gang rape started. Greening went first, and the rest were arguing who was going next. It was John Hunter, followed by Billy Bishop, Peter Reason and Dave Barron. I can still smell them, feel them and the memory makes me feel sick. I knew this moment would never leave me and that I would never live it down.

"I was praying for it to end, and maybe there is a God, as it ended abruptly when Peter Brown burst into the room shouting 'my mum just phoned, she's popping in to pick up some work stuff'.

"The room cleared in what seemed like seconds, but I was unable to leave, as all my clothes had been hidden. Brown made me hide under his bed until his mum left the house. A very long ten minutes later, he returned with my clothes, but that wasn't the end. With his girlfriend out of the way and me in his bedroom naked, he decided to take advantage of the situation. He raped me twice and, unlike Greening, seemed to know what he was doing. With him it was more about sex then humiliation.

"I had always liked Peter Brown and in a perfect world, and had he not been involved with Greening, would have liked him as a boyfriend. It was still rape, but because he wasn't threatening me, calling me names, and nobody was watching, it seemed almost normal. I think that explains what a shit life I had and how messed up I was.

"We agreed what happened between us would remain our secret as both Greening and Chrissie Hudson would not be happy. I kept my word, but months later he told his girlfriend, who went mad, leading to a playground fight witnessed by half the school.

"I won the fight as away from Greening I wasn't a pushover, but I lost the war, as she took great delight in telling everyone why we were fighting. The entire school now knew I was gang raped by Greening and his mates.

"There had been ugly rumours for weeks, but now it was out in the open and confirmed as fact. My reputation was at its lowest. Those incidents became legendary in playground gossip.

"Greening enjoyed humiliating me and revelled in the reputation this bullying behaviour gave him. Boys looked up to him out of fear and girls were just glad they weren't me. If I could turn back time, I would tell my teenage self to be brave and report all those who attacked me. But a combination of fear and embarrassment persuaded me not to report it. It's a decision I've always regretted. If I'd spoken out the first time it wouldn't have happened over and over again.

"When I years later read about the victims coming forward and reporting to Scotland Yard their ordeals 30 years before, I totally understood them. They, like me, had been silent and instead of forgetting the abuse, its left to fester. If I'd spoken up at the start I would have saved myself 6 years of physical abuse and a lifetime of mental torture.

"It would also have meant that Paul Greening would not have become a MP. British politics is dirty and corrupt. The House of Commons is full of liars with massive egos, but even they would not have permitted a known rapist in their ranks. It bothered me for many years that I could have prevented Greening from becoming a member of the establishment.

"The list of disgraced MPs is long and shocking. Politicians from every party have been exposed in the tabloids and locked-up for almost every crime under the sun. But not one in it's 200-year-old history has come close to the depravity of Paul Greening. If the world had known about his secret CV, his life would have been very different. Instead of swaggering around Parliament and appearing on Question Time he would have been placed on the Sex Offenders List. Banged up in Bellmarsh prison or resident in Broadmoor top security hospital.

TEN

Seven Victims

Taylor had not returned to Stanhope since the year of the last attack. Going back to the scene of the crime felt strange, but couldn't be avoided as all but gang leader Greening still lived in the area. She'd traced them on Facebook. Using the alias of Maxine, Taylor struck up a friendship with Greening's former sidekick.

Victim Number One: John Hunter.

The second name on her Hit List and hated almost as much as Tory MP Paul Greening. They exchanged messages and she sucked him in with her fake profile. Within weeks they arranged to meet and the brief encounter would have horrific consequences for the secret sex offender. He had made a terrible decision, as it would end his life.

A mile or so from Basildon New Town, more or less in sleepy Stanhope, was a Premier Inn known locally as 'the knocking shop'. It's where cheating Essex husbands pass the time with other men's wives. Tucked away from the main road, it's discreet and cheap. It's the place where they arranged to meet, and where Hunter dies, in one of the bedrooms. Every woman who has had a fantasy about getting revenge on a man will identify with Taylor.

Taylor told Rebekah:

"Hunter had no idea, and genuinely believed I was Maxine, a bored housewife looking for sex. I hated undressing in front of him but had to convince him I was genuine. When I removed my dress I felt like a slut and looked like a tart in my tacky underwear, but I was playing a role, it was a game I had to play.

"I couldn't stop him looking, but no way was he going to touch me again. He was as arrogant as I remembered, and genuinely believed I was attracted to him. As I removed my skirt and he relaxed on the bed I blurted out 'I'm Taylor Shelley'. There was no reaction, the bastard had wiped my name from his memory and forgotten the 6 years of hell he had put me through.

"I jogged his memory and tweaked his conscience by mentioning Paul Greening. I could see the look of guilt on his face. The penny had dropped, and he suddenly remembered who I was. But it was too late for him to stop the execution.

"When I pulled the knife from my bag I could smell the fear dripping from his pores and it turned me on. Not sexually, but it set off the emotion of hate. He was such a coward, he couldn't look into the eyes of his former victim. I had never killed before and the urge to do so was uncontrollable.

"Without another word, I plunged the knife into his chest and kept on stabbing until I ran out of breath. My mission was accomplished and I didn't want to be in the same room as him any longer.

"As I dressed I couldn't stop smiling, the genie was out of the bottle and I wanted to do it again. It felt so good, seeing one of those who had raped me lying dead in a pool of blood. I placed a copy of the old football team photograph beside his body and left the room.

Victim number two: Billy Bishop.

"He was landlord of The Catcracker pub in Stanhope and advertising on Facebook that he was looking for a new barmaid. I applied for the job and arranged an interview. He suggested 9am, and I agreed as I knew the pub would be empty.

He opened the door with a big smile and invited me in. I followed him into the Saloon Bar and, without warning, plunged the knife into his back. This time there was no conversation and within minutes the deed was done. As he fell to the ground, I stabbed him in the liver, kidney and finally the heart. I placed a photograph of the football team behind the bar, and made my exit."

Victim Three: Peter Brown.

Like Hunter and Brown he still lived in Stanhope and posted on Facebook. Taylor knew what he looked like, so it was easy to track him down. She followed up close for a few days and quickly discovered a pattern. He would be in and out of betting shops, backstreet pubs and a regular in the red light area.

Taylor met Peter Brown in a secluded car park posing as a prostitute. There was no CCTV anywhere near the rundown industrial estate, it had been vandalized months ago. So no evidence of her arriving or plunging the knife into his back.

Victim Number 4: Dave Barron.

A week later Dave Barron is found dead in his blood soaked caravan. He had been stabbed to death and bludgeoned with a hammer.

Taylor recalls:

"He had advertised a caravan for sale so I turned up as an interested buyer. It was over in minutes, there was no need to introduce myself. The minute he turned his back I smashed him with the hammer. The first blow sent him to the ground and shattered his skull at the same time. As he drifted into unconsciousness I stabbed him again and again, enjoying each stab as I entered his flesh and drained his body of blood. I placed the photograph in the caravan bedroom, and said my goodbyes."

Victim Number Five: Casey Newton

He was the Neighbourhood Watch coordinator for his Housing Estate, so, posing as a new resident, she knocked on his front door. She was invited into the lounge and within minutes the carpet was soaked in blood. As with Newton, she smashed the hammer into the back of his head, and finished him off with a single blow to the heart. Again she left the photograph in the house, not too close to the body, but close enough for some to find it and perhaps peace the clues together....or not. She didn't really care. Taylor was now a fuve time murderer and addicted to the art of killing.

Victim number Six: Terry Reason

Reason worked as a Stanhope taxi driver. Taylor despised him because he was driving the white van that 18-year-old Taylor was bundled into before she was gang raped. Greening planned it, but without his involvement it would not have happened. He supplied the vehicle and was the getaway driver. How fitting - his final ride would be driving himself to his own execution.

When the taxi pulled up, Taylor jumped into the back of the smelly cab. Reason still had a hygiene problem and the stench of BO made her want to vomit.

No words were spoken during the ten minute drive to the car park where Billy Bishop was also wiped out.

Once again it was the same MO, with Taylor again attacking unseen from behind, smashing his skull with a hammer and stabbing him in the neck. His throat was cut to ribbons.

She left another photograph in the park but no tip.

Victim Number Seven: Richard Grimson

Grimson had ballooned into a twenty-stone benefit fraudster with mental health problems. He was so out of condition that there was no way he could run away. The only thing he could run was a bath.

So Taylor parked outside his council flat, and as he shuffled past, she jumped out of her car and stabbed him half a dozen times in the back and chest. His life was over in less than 30 seconds, and she drove off with a contented smile on her face.

Now only Paul Greening and David Reynolds remained on her Hit List. Fringe members of the gang Paul Wellings and

Ray Tucker would also be bumped off if she could get to them before the police got to her.

ELEVEN

Serial Killer

Taylor Shelley was now an official Serial Killer who had slayed seven of her abusers. They had got away with multiple rape and, so far, she had got away with mass murder. There were no clues apart from the placing of the same photograph near each body.

Forensic teams had dusted the crime scenes from top to bottom without any luck. There were no fingerprints, DNA or smoking gun. They did find a partial footprint in the muddy ground close to the body of Peter Brown. A high heel estimated to be a size six, but which wasn't considered significant because Essex Police were not looking for a female serial killer, and the print could have been made before the body bled out into the dirt and grime.

Essex Police was no different from any other large organisation. There was always plenty of talk and wild rumours. The Headquarters was a hotbed of petty rivalry, drunken exchanges and false information. Not all Detectives were team players or competent.

DI Charlotte Hawkins was neither. She was a glory hunter with a Helen Mirren haircut and believed she was a real-life Jane Tennyson.

Charlotte was convinced that the first victim would provide the answer as to why these murders had happened. Why they were still happening. A keystone cop or first day rookie at the Hendon Police Training School could work that out. Charlotte Hawkins may be the best-looking female cop in Essex but is certainly not the brightest.

She was correct that the victims were not picked at random, but wide of the mark when telling colleagues "we're looking for a man who hates gays" adding "I believe the victims are all secret homosexuals". She informed local journalist Kelly Baxter "this is a strong possibility."

This bizarre theory, made without a shred of evidence, made the front page of every English tabloid - upsetting relatives, especially the wives, of every victim.

Within hours, the Head of Essex Police had to make a rushed public apology, blaming the story on an unreliable informant. He faced the media, looking flushed and apprehensive, and announced DI Charlotte Hawkins continued to have his full support and that he was confident the murderer would soon be brought to justice.

Adding: "We must assume there's a connection, I don't believe we are dealing with random motiveless murders or that the killings are hate crimes, but at this stage I cannot speculate on the motive. If anybody knows of anybody with a motive, we'd obviously be very pleased to hear about it. You can call us here at the Incident Room, anonymously if you prefer. Make no mistake, we will do whatever it takes to apprehend this man before he has a chance to kill again."

He was, of course, covering his backside. Heaven help him if more dead bodies should turn up on the streets of Stanhope and he'd forgotten to warn the gay community. The truth was that, just like everyone else, he didn't have a clue what was happening on his own patch. And still no suggestion that the killer could be a female.

John Hunter, Billy Bishop, Peter Brown, Dave Baron, Casey Newton, Terry Reason and Richard Grimson had all been murdered, with all their bodies being discovered within a one mile radius. The police wondered and press speculated - were they random killings or targeted for a reason?

Local journalist Kelly Baxter was giving a massive scoop that made it into the national press. A contact in the Stanhope Police force tipped her off about a photograph that was found near the bodies of each victim. The photograph was placed in such a way as to suggest it had been left there as a badly hidden calling card and was not something the victims had lying around. The picture was of the 1981 Stanhope Boys Under 16 Football Team.

Kelly managed to obtain a copy, and discovered one of the team was ultra-right-wing Tory MP Paul Greening. What was the link? Would he be a future victim? What crime, if any, had been committed by those already dead? Who had they upset? What had they all done that was so bad it would end in murder?

TWELVE

Thinking Out Loud

"After the first gang rape, I was putty in their hands and sort of co-operated with everything they wanted. I was gang property. Not because there were eight main members and a few on the fringe, but because, as daft at it sounds, I didn't want to upset them. I didn't want anyone to know what they'd done to me.

"I was terrified and embarrassed about the whole school finding out and being called a 'slag'. They'd remove my clothes and I'd let them again, they could do whatever they wanted, if it meant they'd keep our dirty little secret.

"At first, nobody else knew what had actually happened, and that was all that mattered. There was gossip but because I never complained nobody really believed it. My silence worked for a while, so at least I kept my dignity, but as well as being rapists, bullies and abusers they were also liars.

"Greening started bragging to everyone. The rumours of what went on over at the local park and in that house followed me everywhere. Down the school corridor. In the classroom and on the playground. With my reputation in tatters, my dating days were virtually over. I was branded a 'slag' and no boy wanted me as a girlfriend.

"On Greening's final day at Gable Brook I was frog-marched into the boys changing rooms, stripped naked and made to take a cold shower. But that wasn't the end of my nightmare, as just days before my 18th birthday I was kidnapped by the then 21-year-old Greening and seven members of his old gang. Greening, being Greening, called it a 'school reunion' and wished me 'Happy Birthday'. This incident was worse than everything that happened during my time as a schoolgirl.

"From 13 to 16 I was routinely stripped, humiliated, embarrassed, assaulted and sexually abused by Greening and his gang. Until I was 15, Paul Greening was the only one to rape me. I was always being gang stripped and groped but never gang raped. That was about to change.

"When it started I was 12 and defenceless. He was three years older with a gang to back him up. With hindsight, and as an adult, I can understand why his gang followed him.

At the time I thought he was just a bully. An evil bastard who did what he wanted whenever he felt like it. But he was more than just a psychopath. He was also a larger-than-life character who attracted a loyal following. I'd say half his school gang followed him out of fear, but those who attacked me on the eve of my 18th birthday were his mates. They wanted to be there. Like Greening, they enjoyed gang-raping me.

"I was now both Judge and Jury, and wanted a death sentence for Greening and his co-defendants but my schoolboy abusers will not be wiped-out. They will be punished and I won't let them live.

"I thought it had finally finished on my last day at school but I was wrong. Days before my 18th birthday, I was to suffer my worst and final humiliation."

Taylor saw their van. A battered old white Transit, covered in patches of rust. The back door was open, the engine running. They were going to take her. Gripped with fear, she froze, unable to resist, and was overpowered.

They lifted her off the ground, and bundled her into the back of the van. She endured a young woman's worst nightmare.

"I was grabbed on my way home from work. A white van pulled up alongside me and I froze. Seven men, including Paul Greening, were in the vehicle. Two of them got out, grabbed me by the arms and threw me into the back. It wasn't random, it wasn't a case of me being in the wrong place at the wrong time. What followed proved Greening had planned it down to the last detail. The next few hours would change the rest of her life."

Waiting for her in the van were people she hadn't seen for years, and didn't want to see: Paul Greening, John Hunter, Peter Brown, Dave Barron, Casey Newton, Terry Reason and Richard Grimson. Terry Reason was the driver.

"As the vehicle pulled away Greening and Hunter pinned me to the floor. They were all laughing. The floor of the van was littered with cigarette butts. There must have been a hundred of them, stamped right into the flooring. The smell of smoke and stale beer made my throat close up.

"Within what seemed like 5 or 10 minutes, the van stopped outside a secluded house on the outskirts of Stanhope. They dragged me out of the vehicle and I was pushed through the front door. I was outnumbered by eight to one.

"What followed would be the worst few hours of my life. I started to panic, and felt I couldn't breathe. They were touching me everywhere and wouldn't stop. They were kissing and rubbing me everywhere. And then I felt some fingers going into my vagina.

"All of a sudden my head was pulled to one side by my hair. I tried to pull away but couldn't move. Then Greening ordered them to stop. Just like the old days, he was back in charge and leader of the gang. Everyone backed away. I pulled my top into place and straightened my skirt. There was silence. Eight pairs of eyes staring at me. Some had grins on their faces, others looked threatening.

"I pleaded again and again to be let go, crying as they pushed and pulled me into a bedroom. They stripped me of all my clothes, along with my last shred of dignity. I was about to be treated badly as a young woman by a gang of men.

"It would be far worse than anything that occurred during my time at Gable Brook Comprehensive. Then, it was all about power, bullying, humiliation, intimidation and embarrassment.

It wasn't sex - it was more mental torture and sadistic abuse. This was all about sex.

"The 21-year-old Greening was far more nasty, dangerous and evil than the teenage version. Greening is first. The rest of the gang take their turn, despite my crying and begging them to stop. They ignore my pleading and continue to laugh and jeer throughout my ordeal. At times I was sobbing hysterically. They'd seen the 14, 15, and 16 year-old me naked or half-naked more times than I care to remember. Six of them had previously raped or ganged raped me during our time at Gable Brook Comprehensive, but this was far worse.

"This was different as I was just days away from my 18th birthday. I was an adult, a young woman with a good job and a proper boyfriend. I wasn't the scared schoolgirl that Greening bullied from the age of twelve. But he still considered me worthless.

"They continued switching places and taking turns. The ones that were waiting their turn were rubbing my breasts and sucking my nipples. This was a violent gang rape, far worse than anything that happened before. I knew they would be locked up for a very long time if I found the courage to go to the police, and so did they.

"When they had all finally finished, Greening started messing with my head. He made threats that convinced me not to go the police. Did I really want my boyfriend to know? Who would believe my version? They would all say I consented to everything, and twisted the knife, saying 'we'll get everyone to tell what you was like at school and all the things you did. We'll fucking destroy you. Do you want to take that chance?'

"Of course I didn't, and Greening knew that, so I agreed to keep my mouth shut and was given my clothes back. They drove me back to Stanhope Town Centre, and as I got out of the van I promised myself that one day I would make them all pay. At the time I didn't know it would take me Thirty years.

"It was the last time any of them physically abused me, but not their final act. Greening had one more trick up his sleeve. A few months later, I was with my boyfriend in a central

London pub, and 25 miles from Stanhope. I was on a night out and thought I was safe. Wrong.

"Who should walk in but Paul Greening, John Hunter, Billy Bishop and Casey Newton. I was mortified. They spent the next twenty minutes staring at me and trying to buzz me out. I was terrified of them coming over and knew they were waiting for an opportunity to pounce.

"As soon as my boyfriend got up to go to the gents, Greening came over. He was grinning like a Cheshire cat, said 'hello' and whispered 'be outside in 5 minutes' adding 'do it or we'll have a word with your boyfriend'. I knew exactly want he meant, and he knew I knew.

"My boyfriend came back to the table and I pretended I needed the loo. I went outside, where Greening was waiting He assumed it was business as usual and that I would comply. The threats started, but didn't scare me. I decided to make a stand.

"Greening said unless I went with him, he'd tell my boyfriend everything. I refused. He then said unless I met him the next day, he'd have a word with my boyfriend. This time I shrugged and said 'fine'. I didn't mean it, but I said it. This threw him, and he walked off saying 'Watch yourself when you're back in Stanhope'.

"I was as shocked as him that at last I'd found the courage to stand up to him, but I knew it wouldn't be that easy to escape his clutches. He wasn't joking when he threatened 'watch yourself'.

"Back in Stanhope, on his turf, in his manor, I would be in real danger. I decided to take drastic action. Starting a new life where nobody knew me seemed like a good idea to me. So, at 18, I moved away from Stanhope and spent 10 years travelling all over the UK and Europe looking for love, highs and peace of mind.

"I would fake being happy. I always tried my best to pretend everything was normal. It didn't work. I never even fooled myself, as I couldn't cope without drink or drugs. At different times I lived both promiscuous and celibate lifestyles looking for salvation. But never found a cure. I would pretend to be someone else, or something else.

"As a teenager I just wanted to be like all the other girls, and as a young woman a mother and a wife. But, it was not to be, as to put it bluntly `I was just so fucked up`."

THIRTEEN

Birthday Blues

"As another year passed, I tried my best to move on and forget, but every time I opened a birthday card the memories came flooding back. People would say "Happy Birthday" and instead of feeling good I would have flashbacks of Paul Greening. My moods would change from anger to depression. I wanted revenge but didn't know how to get it.

"After the final gang rape, I survived by moving away and losing myself in a world of music and Mod culture. I tried to block out my past by drinking heavily and taking drugs. I dealt with my disgusting secret without therapy or professional help by self-medicating.

"I have lived with the shame and consequences of their actions for the past 30 years. The emotional repercussions have been enormous. Soon after the last and final attack I attempted suicide, but I never told a soul my secret. The gang, however, bragged about the 'Eight up' as they put it.

"It wasn't seen as rape, though, it was just a 'gang bang' with me as the ninth member of the gang. I was never a willing member of their gang, either at school or days before my 18th birthday.

"Their gang was all about beating up weaker boys and subjecting girls like me, Janice Lamb and Tina Thompson to humiliating, degrading sexual acts. They just saw us as slags and willing participants in group sex.

"At the time I didn't know it happened on council estates and inner-city neighbourhoods up and down the country. Nowadays there are stories every week about gang culture where gang rapes are a form of initiation. But back in the 80s it was unknown.

"I have suffered from depression, panic attacks, nightmares and many symptoms of post-traumatic disorders ever since. At the same time, Paul Greening was re-inventing himself as a respectable Tory politician. He felt no guilt and had no concern for my suffering or my feelings. That is why he had to die.

Taylor had killed 7 times without any help or the knowledge of on/off boyfriend Harry Harris. But she knew murdering Paul Greening had to be special and required expert help. Who better than a career criminal and gangland enforcer obsessed with her? Once she told Harry what she had done and her reasons, he was furious at Greening. He chopped out a massive line of coke and promised, "You have my word. The bastard is dead meat."

24 hours later, the MP would be thrown into the back of a van and taking his last ever journey... a drive that would end in his death. The perverted rapist was facing the final curtain.

When Greening pulled up outside his mock Tudor mansion in his flash BMW, Harry and his Hammers were waiting. The magnificent five, all tooled up and ready to rumble.

A slightly drunk Greening staggered towards the house but didn't make it to the safety of his front door. His path was blocked by a grinning and coked-up Harry Harris. At first his manner was almost business-like, but Harry could tell he was scared. Greening was a typical politician, a good actor, and a liar, but he was rattled. He thought it was a mugging and didn't realise it was a kidnap that would end in his demise.

Confronted by Harry, his loyal lieutenant Turbo and Mike Tyson lookalike Warwick Courtney, he whimpered:

"Please don't hurt me! Take my wallet, take the car."

Career criminal Harry is insulted at being mistaken for a common thief, and makes a mental note to deal with this offensive remark at a later date.

The dynamic trio are joined by Mad Martin Smith who snarls, "You ain't got a fucking clue mate". A white van pulls up, and the terrified rapist is bundled into the back.

Paul Greening is now the property of gun-toting Harry Harris and his life is about to change forever. It's going to end before he makes another vitriol-filled speech in the House of Commons. As his prison-on-wheels speeds away, the sex fiend is lying face down on a filthy mattress with fear in his heart and a gun at his head.

Warwick, Turbo and Dave Diamond, the youngest member of the gang wearing a black balaclava for dramatic effect, go through his pockets looking for a mobile.

Harry is in the front with getaway driver Mad Martin who shouts "Stop your fucking crying or I'll cut your balls off." Laughs all round.

Harry asks: "Why do you think we snatched you?"

There is silence, except for Greenings whimpering. The gangster is not amused and asks again, this time in a slow and menacing manner.

"When I ask a fucking question you answer. I repeat - why do you think we've snatched you?"

Greening fight back tears and mumbles:

"Is it political?"

He is asked to try again.

"You want money?"

"Nah, not even close, we want your body, you fat bastard." Harry laughed, adding, "We're the Gay Mafia and we want your fat arse for the night - and we're fucking having it"

More laughter as the Tory MP and former rapist bursts into tears. Harry is enjoying himself and continues to mess with his head:

"The thing is, darling, we're a bunch of militant homosexuals, we think you're cute and we're gonna fuck you."

Roars of laughter from all those in the van, apart from the kidnapped politician, crying, sweating and shitting himself.

The fat bastard had spent all his life bullying the weak and vulnerable, taking advantage, ripping-off the poor, now it was his turn to be a victim.

"Turbo - take his fucking trousers down"

The trembling tub of lard is begging them to stop. Scared stiff and, like Taylor Shelly in the past, unable to defend himself. Mad Martin and Diamond hold him down as Turbo unzips and pulls down his pin-stripe trousers.

Greening wets himself.

"You dirty fucking bastard" shouts Turbo. "The slag has pissed all over my fucking hands!"

The Tory MP for Oxford Marshes is punished by a punch in the mouth and a kick in the balls, and spends the rest of the journey wearing soggy Y-fronts and a terrified expression.

He doesn't know it but that was kids' stuff compared to the adult X-rated punishment to come. As anyone with Underworld connections will testify, kosher criminals do not like sex offenders.

The white van pulls up in the alley next to The Ritzy, Harry's East London pole dancing club. It is now a fact that Paul Greening will not be having another Birthday or become leader of the Conservative Party. He is 50 miles away from his safe suburban home and a few hours from death.

Pinned to the entrance at the front of the building is a sign saying 'Closed For Private Party'.

The scared and tearful Tory is dragged out of the van and bundled into the club, where he is blindfolded and beaten.

Paul Greening has no idea what is happening, or why. Unlike Taylor Shelley, he's forgotten his past and what happened all those years ago in Stanhope.

Watching as Greening is tied to a pole in the middle of the stage is a smiling Chloe Anderson. Pleased in the knowledge that her starring role is just moments away. Chloe is the sexiest stripper working in the club and as a child was also abused. So for her it is personal.

She is more than happy to help bring this pervert to justice and make him pay for his sick crimes.

Cutie Chloe thought the punishment would be a severe beating and had no idea she was participating in a dramatic build-up to murder. All she wanted in return for her participation was a night off from stripping for a room full of coked-up city boys. The brunette beauty, a part-time glamour model and occasional porn star, was desperate to get involved.

Greening sobbed and wobbled like a giant pink jelly as he awaited his fate. Sixty minutes earlier he had been drunk, but now he was stone cold sober. The roles had been reversed, and for the first time the life-long abuser was now a victim, but unlike his victims he was not young, sweet or innocent.

"Untie him and take off the blinkers" shouted Harry.

Greening stood frozen to the spot, as three Cockney cowboys pointed guns at every part of his body.

One either side, with Diamond, still wearing his balaclava to instill extra fear, standing right in front of him.

"Get your fucking clothes off" barked Harry, "Strip, you slag" sounding just like the Michael Caine character in the iconic gangster movie Get Carter.

Greening is both begging and foolishly making pathetic threats at the same time. One minute offering them a fortune if they stop, the next threatening to report to the police.

Harry, unimpressed by either the offer of money or threat of old bill, warns;

"I'll count to three and then I'll start shooting"

Tory boy is as white as a sheet and close to throwing up.

"One.... Two...."

There is huge laughter all round as a trembling Greening starts to undress in front of five jeering men and a silent female standing in the wings. The pervert is soon stark bollock naked as the gunslingers make sick jokes at his expense.

Harry orders Martin to pick up his clothes and throw them in a bin, saying "he won't be needing them anymore, not where he's going".

Without stating the obvious, the Tory MP looked scared.

"Down on all fours you fucking muppet", roared Harry.

Greening dropped to the floor whimpering like a stray dog as Chloe and the gang topped up with refreshments. A few lines of Colombian marching powder to prepare for the next phase of punishment. Taylor arrives, just in time to watch Chloe perform.

She doesn't approach her life-long enemy, and instead waits in the wings. Her moment will come, but first she wants to witness his humiliation in private.

The blood drains from Greening's fat face as Harry starts shouting "Gay gangbang. Gay gangbang," before barking out a new set of orders. "Stand up you slag" as Turbo points a video camera at him. "I hope you're photogenic, you ugly bastard"

Much merriment all round, and Chloe breaks her silence and laughs at that one. Harry, sounding like the host of a Saturday night TV show says;

"On the decks is my mate Mad Micky Martin, and when you hear the intro to YMCA you start fucking dancing or I'll stick this microphone right up your fat arse"

The song starts, and Greening starts swaying more through fear than natural rhythm.

"Call that fucking dancing? Do you want my shooter up your fucking arse? Now start fucking dancing, entertain us you fucking bastard"

Such is his heavy Cockney accent and dramatic delivery, it's obvious he`s a big fan of both Ray Winstone and Danny Dyer. For the next three minutes, the red-faced rapist pranced around the stage like an embarrassing dad-dancer on acid. Not a pretty sight, imagine a naked Ed Balls on Strictly Come Dancing.

Every moment is captured on camera to be uploaded onto YouTube. The Tory MP will soon be dead, but never forgotten, as his reputation is destroyed on TV shows like Have I Got News For You and Mock The Week. When the music stops there is no applause.

Harry jokes, "You ain't passed the audition, you ain't got the X Factor, but the job is yours. You're perfect for the role of a corpse."

Disorientated, scared shitless and totally humiliated, Paul Greening is a broken man who has lost the will to live, let alone resist. But before he takes his final breath, far worse is to come. He is going to suffer a fate worse than death, and then death itself.

The punishment would be at the hands of two women from different generations. A 21-year-old pole dancer and a 47-year-old historical sex victim, united by their mutual hatred of perverts. How appropriate that this evil rapist should end his life begging 2 females of the species for mercy.

Greening's hands are tied behind his back. He's secured to a shiny pole with a look of fear on his face and a rope around his neck. The rope is deliberately tight so it's impossible for him to look away from what is about to be put in front of him.

Chloe is about to join the party. The opening bars of Rod Stewart's 'Do You Think I'm Sexy' boom out of the sound system as she emerges from the shadows dressed in tacky underwear.

Chloe struts her stuff inches from his shaking beer belly, limp penis and bad breath. She removes her clothes and spits in his face. Chloe is so sexy that even a tied-up and terrified Greening can't fail to be aroused.

This is why Harry asked her dance. "You can look, fat boy, but you can't touch."

The dirtiest dancer in East London removes her bra, pulls down her G-string and wraps her legs around his fat sweaty body. She then drops to her knees and puts her mouth inches from his manhood, teasing but not touching.

How much more can the Tory MP take before he explodes? The answer is not a lot. Chloe lies on her back, gyrates in front of him, spreads her legs and touches his penis with her stockinged foot. The over-excited sex abuser can contain himself no longer and embarrassingly ejaculates over her foot.

"Got it" shouts Harry, "All on tape, great stuff, the papers will love that"

He mocks, "You ain't gonna be Prime Minister, but you will be an internet sensation"

The naked Chloe couldn't resist one more punch, before spitting in his face and kicking him in the balls. That was for Taylor and for the sexual abuse she suffered as a 13-year-old at the hands of a scummy uncle.

"Thanks Chloe, now put your knickers on, get yourself a drink and help yourself to some coke." Harry said.

Greening, his complexion gone from deathly white to bright purple, is squirming with embarrassment as everyone revels in his humiliation.

The sexy stripper, still topless sits in front of Greening, determined to make him feel as uncomfortable as possible.

Harry knew Greening was a teenage National Front supporter before becoming a right-wing Tory.

The media would often refer to him as 'A modern-day Enoch Powell'.

It was no secret the life-long white supremacist didn't believe in inter-racial relationships.

"Hey Warwick - give Chloe a kiss, that will really piss him off" shouts Harry.

They embrace, inches from his face. Chloe holds a lighter close to Greening's penis and threatens to burn it off for 'cumming his whack' all over her foot. There are nine people in the room but only eight are laughing.

Harry gives her a peck on the cheek saying: "Nice one babe, get yourself dressed and order a cab."

She wants to stay, but is told 'things are going to get heavy, so best you leave'.

Impressed by her performance, the grinning gangster gives her the week off on full pay.

The rest of the gang will soon be leaving the building, as the main event is just moments away.

FOURTEEN

The Final Solution

Only the main players remain. A fired-up Harry, a terrified Greening, and star of the show Taylor Shelley. This is her moment.

Harry hands her a baseball bat saying: "Just enjoy it babe, enjoy your revenge."

Taylor told the police the original plan was to kill him really quickly, but now she wasn't keen. She had dramatically changed her mind. The 7-time killer knew that a quick execution wouldn't be enough to bring her closure. She needed answers to thirty years of questions that had been rattling around in her head. Those voices were now saying 'Before you kill the bastard, make him talk'.

There was no rush. He wasn't going anywhere. Escape wasn't an option. He was tied up, couldn't move and was both a dead duck and sitting target.

"I thought - before beating the shit out of him, get the answers you need. Ask why he did all those horrible things".

Taylor agreed with the voices in her head. She wouldn't kill him straight away and instead make him suffer, just as he had her.

The Tory MP was a prisoner, trussed up like a turkey in an East End strip club. He was stark bollock naked and tied to a pole in the middle of a strip club. How the mighty fall.

His big hero Enoch Powell once famously said "All political careers end in failure". The racist Tory Icon was wrong with his infamous 'rivers of blood' quote, but got it right about all political careers ending in failure: Maggie Thatcher, Tony Blair and Paul Greening.

"He looked terrified and it felt good. After introducing myself I spat in his face. I wanted to kill him there and then, and could have, but instead I listened to the voices in my head. They were saying 'you don't want him dead yet, have a little chat with the perverted pond life'. I agreed. I'd already witnessed his humiliation and the night was young.

"My heart was pounding, my mouth was dry, but he wasn't going anywhere, so no rush to put him out of his misery just yet. I'd waited 30 years for this moment, so what difference would another hour make? I wanted to question him.

"Harry gave me a bottle of water, and then tipped a bucket of urine over Greening's head. I ordered him to answer my questions or else. I enjoyed the power of interrogation. I quizzed him, but not like a QC or a 'Rumpole of the Bailey' - my approach was more 'Mad Frankie Fraser'.

"I didn't have any pliers, but warned him - every time I was met with silence or he lied, I'd slash his face with a Stanley knife. It didn't start well, as straight away he blamed it all on the others. He even claimed John Hunter was the leader, so I slashed him across the face. A deep gaping wound that stretched from one ear to the other.

"Had he forgotten I was there? I was the teenage girl he used and abused for 6 years. I saw red, so I slashed him again, this time across the chest and the blood poured out like water from a burst pipe.

"It was turning into an East End version of the Nuremberg Trials, which, unknown to Greening, would end in a Saddam-style execution.

"I reached for my phone, as I wanted his confession recorded and on-the-record. He'd had enough death by a 1000 cuts, and for the next hour admitted all the charges.

"Yes he raped me aged 14, 15, 16 and 18. Yes he bullied, sexually abused, humiliated and terrified me for almost 6 years. This included gang rape, stripping me naked at school, behind the youth club, in the local park and forcing me to steal. I made him say 'you wasn't a slag and I'm sorry'.

"He admitted I was never a willing participant and that it was all his fault. Those were the last words to come from his mouth, followed by hysterical screams as I plunged my knife into his heart. I'd heard enough, and continued to cut him to bits with the Stanley knife, before finishing him off with a baseball bat.

"I smashed him around the body, cracked his kneecaps and broke his hands and feet. I wanted to kill him and I did. The monster had been slain, and my demons released.

"Harry embraced me like a character from The Godfather and I felt like a member of the Mafia. He ordered me to leave on the hurry up, so I fled what many would call the scene of a crime, though I didn't, and still don't believe I did anything wrong. "I'll sort out an alibi and clean up here" promised Harry.

"So I said my goodbyes and left. Hours after the execution, the adrenalin was still pumping as I relived every moment.

"Three days later I pick up a copy of The Sun and couldn't stop laughing. Headline: TORY MP FOUND MURDERED

"The opening lines brought a big smile to my face and joy to my heart. They revealed he'd been found naked with multiple knife wounds, and a black stocking in his mouth. Would I ever stop smiling? I didn't just kill him - I had the added pleasure of destroying his reputation."

Later, as Taylor is having a celebration drink in her local wine bar, Harry swaggers in looking every inch the modern day gangster - dark glasses, cropped hair and a boxer's face. Designer suit and swathed in gold. A soppy grin on his face but still oozing more menace than a hungry Rottweiler.

He whispers in her ear: "The fucking pervert won't be bothering you again."

FIFTEEN

Guilty but Free

Taylor took many secrets to her grave and some I will share with you. It wasn't just her who got away with murder. I,m glad to say, Harry and the others all got away with the murder of Paul Greening.

No names were mentioned in her confession to the police or interview with Rebekah. The police had no idea she'd murdered the Tory MP in a lap dancing Club. Taylor refused to say where she had executed him, and they didn't have a clue.

She admitted to all eight murders, and insisted she acted alone. Not once, during hours of questioning, did the police mention Harry Harris or The Ritzy Club.

There was not even the flimsiest finger of suspicion. There was nothing to link an East End gangster with a Tory politician.

It wasn't like Ronnie Kray and Tory Peer Lord Boothby in the 1960s, there were no photographs for the Daily Mirror to publish.

Taylor wasn't named as a suspect on SKY News - so why did she hand herself in? She wanted the world to know the truth, and the opportunity to explain why she became a serial killer.

She'd already confessed to journalist Rebekah Woods, but wanted her day in Court. The guilty eight were dead but the truth would only come out if she went on trial.

She had everything to gain and nothing to lose. Taylor would swear on the bible and tell her story from the Witness Box at the Old Bailey.

It would be reported on every TV news bulletin and for weeks would be on the front page of every tabloid.

She could destroy the reputation of a Tory MP, and at the same time maybe become a martyr for the cause of battered and bullied women - a pin-up for female victims of sexual abuse and domestic violence.

She also knew she'd never be punished, and in a way would get away with murder. The police and the authorities didn't know her secret. When the jury found her guilty the old Etonian Judge almost had an orgasm as he dreamed of sentencing her to life imprisonment. As we know...she was dying of cancer with just months to live.

"When I entered the Witness Box I was wearing my Sunday best and done up to the Nines. I wore designer shoes, and a Victoria Beckham dress with a little too much make-up. I was determined to look a million dollars and gave the tabloids exactly what they wanted.

"All eyes were fixed on me. I spotted Rebekah in the Press Box, Harry in the gallery and D.I Charlotte Hawkins at the back of the court.

"I could tell that the Judge was not amused and had a very low opinion of me, but why should I care? I wasn't there to influence or impress him. What was the point? I was guilty. I would plead guilty. I would proudly plead guilty.

"For me the Old Bailey trial was all about exposing the vile and perverted past of Paul Greening MP - the naming and shaming of his gang.

"I would be found guilty, but knew I'd soon be free. My legal Team, the Judge, Rebekah Woods, Harry Harris, not a soul knew what I knew. Three months before starting my killing spree I was told by a Harley Street doctor that I was dying of cancer. I only had weeks to live. I was going to defeat British Justice and stick two fingers up to the Establishment. That is why I smiled more then I cried in the Witness Box. Reliving the rapes and sexual abuse was extremely painful, but eased by pubically destroying the reputation of Paul Greening.

It wasn't just my day in court. It was much more. I knew I was going to have the last laugh"

SIXTEEN

The Last Hurrah

Taylor talks about the hours before her arrest.

"My last night of freedom was spent in a top London hotel snorting cocaine, drinking champagne and making love to Harry Harris. He slipped off at dawn and then at mid-day I handed myself over to Essex Police.

"My arrest was stage-mannered and witnessed by a Sun photographer and Sky News. It would be my last-ever public appearance.

"I was wearing my Sunday best with perfect make-up and not a hair out of place as I knew the pictures would be flashed all around the world It was my last chance to acquire cult status, and let's be honest, everyone loves a pretty face. Even if it belongs to a serial killer.

"During the interview it soon became clear that Essex police had no idea why I'd become a serial killer. They were baffled. They didn't have a clue about what linked me to the boys in the football photo. They had worked out they all went to Gable Brook School, that was easy, but not the connection to me. Though, to be fair, how could they? Who would suspect a 47-year-old female with a Thirty-year grudge? Why would a law-abiding hairdresser with a chain of salons become a serial killer?

"The interviewing officers were shocked when I confessed, and disbelieving when I told them why. Most high-ranking coppers are middle class and Conservative Party supporters. Paul Greening was hard-line on law and order, the darling of

83

the Police Federation. He had become one of them, and they couldn't believe there political hero was a former rapist. It was only after speaking to others in the photograph and former pupils at Gable Brook that, little by little, they started to believe me.

"Tory MP Paul Greening, the law-abiding member of society and respectable pillar of the community, had a criminal past. Over the years loyalties change, and many people came out of the closet and confirmed his past as a teenage thug. He was also a serial rapist, a bully and a racist. They also confirmed that the seven other victims were also teenage gang members, rapists and bullies.

Taylor told the police her only regret was that three members of the gang had gone unpunished. Two, Paul Wellings and Ray Tucker, were fringe members, but David Reynolds had once raped her. He escaped her knife because she couldn't trace him on Facebook, Twitter or the Electoral Roll.

Luckily for them their lives were spared - but not their reputations. Taylor destroyed those when giving evidence at her Old Bailey trial.

They were then crucified by the world's media, who'd set up camp in Stanhope and chased them all over Essex.

After her courtroom revelations there was much activity. Armed police with arrest warrants kicked down doors and tabloid journalists flashed their cheque books in pubs all over Essex.

Gossip, facts and unfounded rumours spread like wildfire as friends and enemies delved into the background of Paul Greening. The three gang members who escaped death, and the vengeance of Taylor Shelley, were not so lucky with official justice.

Paul Wellings 50, Ray Tucker 50, and 49-year-old David Reynolds were all arrested and charged with committing historical crimes.

Reporting restrictions were lifted and the cat was out of the bag. The media were comparing them and the Tory MP to Jimmy Saville, Rolf Harris and Gary Glitter.

Taylor Shelley was to stand trial for 8 murders, but it was the dead Tory MP and the three that got away who were the most hated men in the country. So much so that, for their own safety, they were remanded in custody.

Taylor talks from prison about her arrest with journo Rebekah Woods:

"I was treated like Public Enemy Number One, surrounded by cops and medical staff from the Criminal Mental Health Service. I thought to myself `do they think I`m mad?` They inform me I`m a danger to society.

"It was obvious they saw me as a cold blooded killer rather then a victim. Apparently I have `mental problems` which is news to me, they do say you learn something new every day. But I was not convinced."

Being locked-up had not dented her sense of humour, on the contary, if anything Taylor seemed to be in a good frame of mind. Killing Paul Greening had made her genuinely happy. She didn't seem bothered by the prospect of a Life Sentence for mass murder. Perhaps she knew something we didn't know?

"My arrest was like something out of One Flew Over The Cuckoos Nest with me in the Jack Nicholson role. I was interviewed for about 90 minutes by the white coat brigade and then banged up in a freezing cold underground cell.

"A few hours later I`m taken from my windowless cave by half a dozen burly cops for a cosy little chat in another tomb of a room. I`m thinking it aint like this in the films. Where is my brief and what about my phone call. They are treating me more like a political prisoner then a women with a genuine grievence"

Have the authorities got her sedated? Is Taylor on medication or has the noteriety gone to her head? She appears to be more ballsy, confident and cocky then any other time in her life. Or is she genuinely elated, like an Olympic Champion or a Everest Mountain climber, that she has achieved her life-long ambition? The slaughter of Paul Greening and his gang.

"Two plain-clothed detectives enter the room, a moronic male and a pretty female of the species. Mister Plod was Fred Flinstone without the loincloth and it`s pretty obvious that Lady Cop models herself on Prime Suspects Jane Tennyson. I am face to face with a caveman cop and a wannabee Charlie`s Angel.

"They tried to engage me in conversation but for over a hour I stuck to 'no comment' and amused myself by imagining the male cop in a Tutu. Fred Flinstone lacked the wit and charm of a waxwork dummy and she didn't have the brains to go with her looks. We are talking `Dumber and Dumber`. She was dead cute but he was brain dead.

"Cutie played good cop and Freddie acted the heavy, but I wasn't impressed with there performances. To be honest he was more B movie extra than a Oscar winner and she was nothing more then a pretty face. God help us if there ever asked to investigate a proper crime and find the culprit."

Taylor has a point, she has already confessed to eight murders. Rebekah was shocked at her change of personality. At the hotel she was proud of what she`d done and showed no remorse. But now she was both Cocky, and considering her circumstances suprisingly upbeat and happy. Maybe becoming a serial killer was the cure for her life-long depression.

"The truth is they didn't land a glove on me. There was no knockout punch and I won every round on points It was so easy and I got bored with all there questions and saying `no comment` to everything , I decided to piss them off by saying `I only talk to the press`.

"They genuinely thought I was bonkers and I found myself handcuffed, bundled into a meat wagon bound for Holloway Prison. And here I am still here three weeks later."

Was Taylor Shelley cracking up? Enjoying the attention that goes with being a serial killer? Or had she cleansed her soul?

SEVENTEEN

The Last Word

The interview with Rebekah was a double-edged sword. Taylor gave up her right to anonymity, but it guaranteed Greening and the others would be publically named and shamed.

When her trial started at The Old Bailey it was a media sensation. The biggest court case since the OJ Simpson murder trial, or when Oscar Pitorius was accused of murdering his girlfriend.

It was a media circus - on the front page of every tabloid and covered by television crews from around the world.

The proceedings were discussed daily on every TV show, from Good Morning Britain to Loose Woman to The Daily Politics. It was the talk of every pub and bus stop. The nation was gripped, and also divided.

Taylor Shelley was a self-confessed serial killer, but not a universal hate figure Apart from hard-line Tory voters, and assorted perverts, the majority of the great British public were either on her side or at least had sympathy.

This was a woman who, as a teenage girl, was raped and abused by a violent gang led by a future Conservative MP.

Much to the Judge's disgust, the court of public opinion had already cleared her of murder. They considered it a form of self-defence.

Rock Bands were writing songs, punk poets performing rants in her defence and Camden Market shops selling T-Shirts bearing her name or picture. The most popular with 'Serial Killer' emblazoned across the front in white letters on a black background. But Taylor was not going to walk free.

In court she looked heroic in the Witness Box and sounded vulnerable when she spoke, but the establishment was against her. They wanted her head on a plate, but Taylor would have the last laugh.

Members of the jury and hard-bitten hacks in the Press Gallery were close to tears as she told of the crimes inflicted on her by Paul Greening and his gang.

The details were truly shocking - a catalogue of sexual abuse carried out over a 6-year period. But the establishment would punish her for taking the law into her own hands. Or would they?

A "Not Guilty" verdict was not on the cards but did she have a "Get Out Of Jail" card up her sleeve?

If the Death Penalty still existed, unlike Ruth Ellis, the last woman to hang in the UK, would Taylor have escaped the hangman's rope? In a sensational twist, the legal system and British establishment were denied the opportunity to crucify her.

Taylor died in her sleep hours after the jury returned its verdict, but hours before the Judge could pass sentence. The sadistic Judge, an old Etonian and fox hunting Tory, was not happy. Without a single expression of compassion for her suffering he dismissed her as a "dangerous and evil woman".

The same Judge had, a year earlier, attacked the victim in a rape case for wearing a short skirt and revealing top.

Implying she had "asked for it".

He was that sort of bastard Judge.

A fascist from the Shires who slept with prostitutes, visited sex dungeons and beat his wife.

The old duffer was furious that Taylor Shelley had escaped his draconian form of justice.

As he showed in his biased summing up, bragging in his public schoolboy accent "I would have sentenced the accused to life in prison without parole".

Taylor was due to give evidence in the case against her three surviving abusers. David Reynolds, Paul Wellings and Ray Tucker.

All had been charged with various acts of violence including, rape, sexual abuse, kidnapping, false imprisonment and threatening behaviour.

Taylor Shelley wasn't alive to give evidence in person, the Tory MP was dead, so on legal advice they blamed everything on Greening and the others.

They all claimed Taylor Shelley was the school slag and that Paul Greening forced them to take part in what they called 'consensual group sex'.

Like Taylor, the perverted politician wasn't alive to defend himself.

Under cross-examination they admitted sexual activity with Taylor but denied being rapists.

The Judge went out of his way to clear them, and bent over backwards to persuade the jury to find them 'not guilty'.

They weren't just given the benefit of every doubt, they were virtually coached on how to best answer each question by the so-called learned judge.

It was vitally important for the establishment to discredit Taylor Shelley and protect the reputation of Paul Greening, and his father-in-law Sir Roderick Pratt-Dawson. In their eyes, she was a worthless working class slag and not worthy of compassion.

The fact she was an innocent victim of a sex gang was virtually forgotten. She was a bottle-blonde serial killer from a council estate, whereas Greening was a Tory MP with friends in high places.

The Judge managed to swing the jury and fix the result with a 'not guilty' verdict, but he could not the corrupt the court of public opinion.

Disgusted next-door neighbours, friends and even some family members were not convinced of their innocence. Their reputations were destroyed and they all suffered a backlash on the street.

90

One was disowned by his wife, another beaten up in his local pub and David Reynolds eventually took his own life. At least one of them had a conscience and the guts to do the decent thing.

It may not be politically correct to say it out loud, but maybe Taylor Shelley did the right thing by taking the law into her own hands.

The last thoughts of Taylor Shelley were passed onto the world by Kate Chambers, a fellow con, who shared her final hours. Released just weeks after her cellmates death Kate was wanted by every media outlet in the UK. Her story will be told in the sequel to this book.

ACKNOWLEDGEMENTS

Teddie Dahlin
Sandie West
Rebekah Wade

My Mum & Barry
Garry Bushell
Matthew Worley
Vere Bishop

Soren Sulo Karlsson
Kevin Poree

Paul & Diane
Justine & Jim
Kelly & Ricky
Rob & Jodie

Tim Wells
Sophie Cameron
John Dryland
Hughie Gadson

Dr Sims
Basildon Hospital
Professor Eghan Khan for saving my life
and
DAVID BOWIE the person who inspired me to be creative in
the first place
not forgetting
Erica Echenberg who back in the day predicted I had the
talent to become a writer

Lightning Source UK Ltd.
Milton Keynes UK
UKOW05f0633120417
298942UK00017B/534/P